Tipbook Music for Kids and Teens

A Guide for Parents and Caregivers

D1738830

Publishing Details

This first edition published 2006 by
The Tipbook Company bv, The Netherlands.

Typeset in Glasgow and Minion.

Printed in The Netherlands by drukkerij Wilco, Amersfoort.

© 2006 THE TIPBOOK COMPANY BV

216 pp

ISBN 90-76192-50-2

Hugo Pinksterboer

Tipbook Music for Kids and Teens

A Guide For Parents And Caregivers

Handy, clearly written, and always up-to-date.

The guide for parents who want to make informed decisions on the musical education of their children. Includes Tipcodes!

Thanks!

For their information, inspiration, expertise, time, and help, we'd like to thank the following musicians, educators, parents, and other national and international experts: Steve Clover, Sherise Parker-Alofs, Maribeth Barrons, Davina Cowan, Bob Wendel (Robert Wendel Music, NY), Graham Lyons, Guntram Wolf (instrument maker, Germany), Hugo Rodriguez (Antigua Winds), Eugene Monnig (Cadenza Music, Minnesota), Ron Payne (Music Teacher Magazine), Jojo Mayer, Henk Rensink, Bert Steinman, Albert van Ee, Mia Dreese (NFG, Dutch Flute Association), Lies Vledder (European String Teachers Association), Ad van Dun, Maarten Visser (Flutelab), Ruud van der Meulen (Probasse), Jan van den Eijnden (Unisono), and the dozens of experts who contributed to the educational issues in the first fourteen Tipbooks.

Anything missing?

Any omissions? Any areas that could be improved? Please go to www.tipbook.com to contact us. Thanks!

The makers

Journalist, writer, and musician **Hugo Pinksterboer**, author of *The Tipbook Series*, has published hundreds of interviews and articles, as well as instrument, video, CD, and book reviews for national and international music magazines.

Illustrator, designer, and musician **Gijs Bierenbroodspot** has worked as an art director for a wide variety of magazines and has developed numerous ad campaigns. While searching in vain for information about saxophone mouthpieces, he got the idea for this series of books on music and musical instruments. He is responsible for the layout and illustrations for all of the Tipbooks.

Concept, design, and illustrations: Gijs Bierenbroodspot
Cover photo: René Vervloet
Editor: Michael J. Collins

IN BRIEF

Playing a musical instrument is a fun, inspiring, and rewarding pastime. It can be a demanding pastime as well, for both children and you, their parents or caregivers. It's also a hobby that requires many small and large decisions: which instrument to play, buying or renting an instrument (and should it be new, or pre-owned?), which teacher to go to, whether to take exams or go to competitions, when to practice, how to keep on practicing, how not to bother neighbors and housemates…

Just that
While the answer to many of these questions may come naturally, it is good to have easy access to well-founded, unbiased, and accessible background information on these and all related subjects. *Tipbook Music for Kids and Teens* is just that.

The same idea
Rather than presenting one professional's opinion on the subject, *Tipbook Music for Kids and Teens* provides you with the insights, ideas, and experiences of various music teachers and other experts whose opinions may sometimes strongly differ — but in the end, they all promote the same idea: Let the children play music!

Hugo Pinksterboer

CONTENTS

VIII   SEE AND HEAR WHAT YOU READ WITH TIPCODE
www.tipbook.com
The Tipcodes in this book give you access to short
videos and sound files at www.tipbook.com. Here's
how it works.

1   CHAPTER 1. MUSIC? MUSIC!
Music is believed to make you smarter; it is both fun
and relaxing; it can help you make friends, and it
enhances both your social skills and your self-
esteem. Plenty of reasons to take your child's musical
education seriously!

8   CHAPTER 2. PHASES AND STYLES
A quick look at the main phases of musical development, and children's learning styles.

18   CHAPTER 3. LEARNING TO PLAY
All aspects of learning to play an instrument, or sing:
from music programs for infants to professional
education, group teaching versus private teaching,
where to find a good teacher and how to recognize
one, costs, and much more.

63   CHAPTER 4. PRACTICING
Learning to play an instrument requires practice —
and practice isn't always fun. Helpful hints on how to
make practicing effective and entertaining, practice
facilities and tools, hearing protection, sound insula-
tion, and more.

93   CHAPTER 5. GUIDANCE & MOTIVATION
Tips on how to keep children playing music.

100   CHAPTER 6. BORROWING, RENTING,
OR BUYING?
Essential information on how and where to get an
instrument for your child, and on the additional costs
of playing an instrument.

117 CHAPTER 7. WHICH INSTRUMENT?
Choosing the right instrument is essential for long-lasting musical fun.

138 CHAPTER 8. PLAYING TOGETHER
The importance of making music in a group, and a quick guide to the main types of bands, orchestras, and other groups.

153 CHAPTER 9. THE INSTRUMENTS
An introduction to the most popular and some lesser-known instruments.

173 CHAPTER 10. BEING PREPARED
Helpful hints to reduce audition anxiety, exam nerves, and stage fright.

182 GLOSSARY

184 TIPCODE LIST
All Music for Kids and Teens Tipcodes listed.

185 WANT TO KNOW MORE?
Information about relevant books, magazines, Websites, and other resources.

196 INDEX

200 ESSENTIAL DATA
Four pages for listing important phone numbers, Websites, and other relevant information.

SEE AND HEAR WHAT YOU READ WITH TIPCODE

www.tipbook.com

In addition to the illustrations on the following pages, Tipbooks offer you a new way to see — and even hear — what you are reading about. The Tipcodes that you will come across throughout this book give you access to short videos, sound files, and other additional information at www.tipbook.com.

Here's how it works: On page 155 of this book, there's a paragraph on the many styles of music you can play with a violin. Right above that paragraph it says **Tipcode KIDS-005**. Type in that code on the Tipcode page at www.tipbook.com, and you'll hear a short audio demonstration. Similar audio examples are available on a variety of subjects; other Tipcodes will link to a short video.

Enter code, watch movie

Enter the Tipcode below the movie window on the Tipcode page. In most cases, you'll see images or hear audio within five to ten seconds.

Quick start

The videos, pictures, and sound files are designed to start quickly. If you miss something the first time, you can always repeat them. And if it all happens too fast, use the pause button below the movie window.

Plug-ins

If the software plug-ins you need to view the videos or photos are not yet installed on your computer, you'll

First, make your selection: Tipcode, chords, and fingering charts, or the glossary.

The Tipcode window displays movies, photo series, fingering charts, chords, and explanations of the words used in this book.

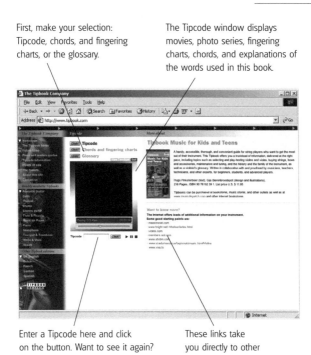

Enter a Tipcode here and click on the button. Want to see it again? Click again.

These links take you directly to other interesting sites.

automatically be told what you need and where you can download it. This kind of software is free.

Still more at www.tipbook.com

You can find even more information at www.tipbook.com. For example, you can look up words in the glossaries of *all* the Tipbooks. There are chord diagrams for guitarists and pianists; fingering charts for saxophonists, clarinetists, and flutists; and rudiments for drummers. Also included are links to some of the Websites mentioned in the *Want to Know More?* section of each Tipbook.

1. MUSIC? MUSIC!

Playing music, on any instrument and in any style, is one of the most rewarding hobbies a child can pick. Playing music enhances your creativity, teaches you problem solving and trains your memory, helps make you smarter, and improves your socials skills. In short, children who learn to perform music are likely to perform better in many aspects of life. That makes music more than just a way to pass time: It is considered an essential element of your child's education.

Providing children with a musical education is much more than actively introducing music into their lives. It truly helps educate them in every sense of the word. As a parent, you have a crucial role in the musical success of your children, whether they want to play an instrument or sing just for fun, or become a professional musician — or both.

Their choice
Many children are naturally and deeply drawn to playing music; if so, you'll have a hard time stopping them. They know what they want to play and will beg for an instrument and music lessons, either because they think it will be fun, or because their friends do it and they want to be part of the action, or for any number of reasons. Many other children, however, may not think about it until you, the school's music teacher, or someone else suggests it to them. At that point, they may be just as enthusiastic and self-motivated, but chances are they'll need more support and guidance.

Or yours

Some parents, rather, decide for their children, getting them piano lessons at age six, or violin lessons at age four, for example. No questions asked, no explanations given; music lessons are simply presented as an inherent part of the child's education, much like going to school.

Not a fad

No matter how children start their musical 'careers,' your guidance and support is essential. If you think music is a vital aspect of their education — as many professionals do — you may take your children to special music programs long before they can talk, or even walk. Or you can choose to just wait and see what happens, and be there when your child is ready. It is very important that you resist any temptation to believe that your child's desire to play music is nothing more than a fad (by doing so, you risk influencing your child to think likewise), or to force your children to play no matter what. Children should primarily associate playing music with fun, rather than with the many duties they otherwise face — which doesn't mean you should allow them to neglect practice just because they don't feel like it. Keep them to their part of the deal: They wanted to play this instrument that you purchased for them, and they can't just let go without even trying.

Play or sing

One of the best ways to get your children interested in playing music is to play yourself. Just like your children learn to walk and talk by watching and listening to you, they will develop an interest in music if they see and hear you play from time to time. And if you don't play? Sing to them. You can rest assured that your vocal abilities are absolutely irrelevant; it is your enthusiasm that will inspire them, not the quality of your performance.

At any level

Every child can learn to play music or sing, just like most people can learn to talk or drive a car. Operating computer and video games — which almost all children do — is often more complex than 'operating' a musical instrument. And, when it comes to music, one of the many benefits is that you can enjoy playing at any level. You don't need to be really good in order to play and have fun, whether by yourself or in a musical group of some kind.

Fun

So first of all, making music is about having fun, whether it's playing by yourself, rehearsing with the school orchestra, performing with a marching band, setting up your own rock band, or working out a flute duet with the kid next door.

Smarter

Music is said to make you smarter, too. Research suggests that listening to a Mozart Sonata can improve one's spatial-temporal reasoning, be it for only ten minutes or so*. This type of reasoning, essential for success in math, science, chess, and checkers (and so on) seems to be enhanced long-term by learning to play an instrument. Part of the explanation is that all these activities involve the recognition of certain patterns, and instrumental music instruction stimulates the same area of the brain that processes numbers and equations.

One of the relationships between music and math: Reading music requires an understanding (and may offer a clarification) of fractions. The shape of a note indicates the note's duration; there are whole notes, half notes, quarter notes, eighth notes, etc.

And more

But it doesn't stop there. Students who play a musical instrument score forty to fifty points higher on the verbal and mathematic sections of the SAT, for example (the same goes for students who have been involved with acting or dancing), and evidence suggests that memory is improved.

And yet more

Also, playing music is often about finding different ways to deal with a problem: How to deal with this tricky bit, which fingering works best for this phrase, how to master

*The so-called (and much debated) Mozart Effect.

this new piece, how to memorize this section. This type of training is beneficial in many areas of life. Besides problem solving and analytical skills, playing music can also foster writing skills, while learning to read music may improve speed-reading abilities and concentration. On a physical level, playing an instrument helps children develop fine motor skills, and eye-hand coordination will be improved.

Early start

An early start is often suggested to make things even more effective. Many experts state that it's best if children have their first active music experiences before the age of six or seven. Just listening to music, which can definitely help to raise your child's interest in learning to play an instrument, is not enough; they have to really do music in order to fully experience its benefits. Many expectant parents follow prenatal programs based on the theory that children who are exposed to music while still in the womb tend to be more relaxed, sleep better, are easier to nurse, and develop at a faster rate. In any case, it won't hurt — and if playing music to your unborn child makes you feel good, it'll probably help your baby feel good too.

Social skills

Playing music in a band or an orchestra brings people together, and it helps children connect with others. Bands, orchestras, and choirs are a rich source of new friends, and offer a solid support system for your child as well. As a matter of fact, for many children, the social aspect is the main reason to play an instrument and be in a band at all. So what about children who prefer to be by themselves? No problem. First, various instruments are very well suited for solo music, such as the guitar or the piano. Second, play-along CDs and similar media offer ample opportunity to play any instrument in the context of a 'virtual' band or ensemble — and you can only hope this makes your child want to join a real live band later on. Besides, doing so is more fun in the end, and playing in an ensemble can truly help them overcome or deal with inhibitions.

Teamwork

Teamwork is an essential element for making any type of ensemble succeed. Being in a band or orchestra teaches children how to work on a common task, and helps them to define their role and present their own voice in a smaller or larger group setting. It also teaches them to listen to others, and to tune in to their fellow musicians (in the broadest sense of that word). And if parents or siblings play an instrument or sing as well, making music at home can definitely help bring the family together.

Communication
Music is often described as a universal language (though some say it's neither universal nor a language). It helps bridge gaps between people of different abilities, cultures, ages, and political convictions; and learning to play an instrument allows you a fascinating way to communicate. Your performance can make people feel good, dance, think, relax….

All alone
At the same time, learning to play an instrument is something you do all alone. Positively speaking, this teaches children self-discipline and time management skills; for example, it encourages them to find ways to use their practice time as effectively as possible. Most children need initial or continued guidance on both points, however. While kids usually don't need to be inspired to watch TV or play games, you will probably have to 'inspire' them to practice, from time to time, and help them use their time wisely. Specific tips follow in later chapters.

A stronger self
Playing music helps many children connect with themselves, gain confidence and self-esteem, and overcome shyness. Children who do not dare to speak up may learn how to do so through their instrument, and many have experienced a much easier time with situations such as presenting a paper in class once they've learned to perform music onstage or play scales in front of fellow classmates. Conversely, there are children who need yoga classes or a drama program to help them overcome their musical stage fright (also see page 179).

Creativity
It goes without saying that playing music enhances creativity and provides a great means for self-expression.

It also teaches active, rather than passive, listening (one disadvantage to this, however, is that you may no longer be able to endure a lousy band, while non-musicians wouldn't know the difference). Most musicians — at any level — also develop a higher appreciation of other forms of art. And while music in itself is usually not considered a tool, such as reading, writing, and math, it most definitely helps you to use those tools creatively — at any age!

Relax
Making music helps reduce stress, as do most means of self-expression. Simply listening to music does so too, of course, but playing requires more focus, which definitely helps you forget your worries. Likewise, playing music is a great means of emotional release — you can obviously let off steam by hitting the drums, but also by playing the flute or piano.

Health
Making music is even said to be good for your immune system, increasing the number of disease-fighting cells. These and other benefits of learning to play an instrument can last a lifetime: Senior citizens who play music tend not only to be healthier, but are bothered less by anxiety, depression, and loneliness.

Discipline
Kids involved in music programs are less likely to develop disciplinary problems or drop out of school. Likewise, they tend to be less inclined to turn to drugs, commit crimes, or show antisocial behavior.

Everyone
One of the beauties of music is that virtually anyone can play, including children with physical, mental, or other disabilities (musical instruments can be adapted to accommodate a number of physical impediments). For example, autistic children can use music to communicate. And above all, what counts is not how well you play, but that you just play.

Paint, dance, play ball
So should every child play music? It would be fun,

probably, but only if they really loved to do so. The truth is, however, that some children just don't like playing an instrument or singing, regardless of how happy and smart and healthy and cooperative and desirable they might become as a result. You may want to encourage them to have a go at it anyway, which might be successful. But if they'd rather paint, dance, or play ball, it may be better to let them do just that. After all, many of the benefits of a musical education listed in this chapter also apply to a wide variety of other creative activities and sports.

Your costs

If they *do* want to play music, be prepared to invest in their musical career, in various ways. One way, of course, is financially, as you'll have to pay for lessons, instruments, accessories, and so on. Also, you'll have to help your children set up and maintain a practice routine, keep them motivated when progress is slow or seemingly non-existent, or when other activities seem to grow more attractive. You may have to get them to and from their lessons and performances. And you may have to endure the often discordant sounds of practice: beginning violinists, budding drummers, or trumpeters playing scales are not always fun to listen to… But it's definitely worth it. Have you ever met someone who regrets being able to play an instrument, or sing?

2. PHASES AND STYLES

When growing up, children go through various phases of musical development. This chapter takes a closer look at those phases, and sheds some light on different learning styles. This information can be very helpful in guiding your child's musical education.

Some children have an inherent talent for music. But is there such a thing as a 'non-musical' child? No... Any child can learn to sing or play an instrument. Most so-called 'non-musical' children are simply those who've had no musical education, or who (sadly) simply believe themselves to be non-musical. Unfortunately, children who are told they are non-musical from an early age — usually by caregivers impatient with the time it took these children to sing in tune or to move to the rhythm of a song — are likely to believe such messages, and will purposefully shy away from attempting to learn or explore music.

Too soon?
Basically, you can't expose your child to music too soon. Special music education programs are available for children at any age, from newborns to toddlers and beyond. Quite a number of children start playing a 'real' instrument (mostly violin or piano) as soon as they're five or six years of age, or even younger.

Just listen
Any adult learning a new language knows that it takes a great deal of time and effort to do so. But young children are capable of learning a second language without any noticeable difficulty, and just by listening to it — so it

would seem only logical that they would pick up music just as easily.

Too late?
Still, it's never too late for your child (or yourself!) to learn to play an instrument. Even if starting at fifteen or sixteen, a child should be able to join the school band after four or five months of lessons and some serious practicing. Quite a number of young drummers, bass players, and guitarists join garage bands the same week they first pick up an instrument. Actually, there are numerous professional musicians who started only in their teens; classical players, too, though they usually have their first lessons at a much younger age. More boys than girls first pick up an instrument in their mid to late teens. This is most likely due to the fact that there tend to be more boys than girls in the pop and rock bands that often inspire teenagers to start playing.

Don't make them wait
Tip: When children show an interest in playing an instrument, don't make them wait until the school's music program starts. Instead, find a private teacher and let them have a go at the instrument of their choice…

Too soon
… unless they're not yet physically ready to play that instrument, of course. In that case, try to come up with an alternative that satisfies their desire to play. Chapter 7 tells you all about choosing an instrument.

Pre-birth
Evidence suggests that children respond to music they were exposed to while still in the womb. Do they actually recognize music from those days? Some specialists say they do, but there's still a lot of debate (such theories are difficult to prove). It is clear, however, that fetuses can hear sounds from some sixteen to twenty weeks after conception, and they appear to actually respond to music after about twenty-six weeks. Their perception is limited to lower frequencies, however, as high frequencies and complex sounds are muffled by the amniotic fluid (the fluid in the womb that surrounds the baby). A tip: There

seems to be no need to put speakers on your belly. The womb is a quiet place, and external sounds will travel there. As mentioned in Chapter 1, there are special prenatal programs that claim to stimulate the development of the fetus through sound.

Newborns
Newborn children can soon indicate what music they like. Between three and six months of age, they will actively respond to music and sounds in general, and soon after become aware of where sounds are coming from. Later, during their first year, they may recognize songs they've heard before, and even 'sing' along.

First words
Most babies say their first words between eight (which is very early) and eighteen months. Singing songs to your baby is very likely to boost their language development.

Toy instruments
Between ages one and two, most children become aware of the various types of music. They begin to better articulate their responses to different songs. Also, they start moving to the music in a more coordinated way, and they will produce sounds by hitting things. You can guide this tendency in a musical direction by giving them any of the many children's age-appropriate toy instruments, such as toy drums, shakers, or xylophones, or even a toy piano.

An outline
Around their second birthday, many children start reproducing parts of songs they've heard, though you will be likely to hear more of a general outline than the exact notes and lyrics. Also, they tend to sing along at this age rather than sing by themselves. This implies that you can play an important role by singing with them. Around the age of three, when they begin to learn the lyrics to simple songs, they're likely to sing by themselves. They may also make up their own songs. Also by this age, they will usually be able to distinguish differences in volume (dynamics), pitch (high and low notes), and tempo. Music appreciation classes can help speed up this process, making children more aware of these concepts.

Real lessons

As children grow older, they will develop an awareness of pitch and rhythm and learn to distinguish the sounds of different instruments. The scope of the songs they can sing increases as their vocabulary expands and they gain more control over their vocals. Likewise, their motor skills, coordination, and ability to focus will increase to a point where they get ready for their first 'real' music lessons — 'real' meaning they learn to really play a bona fide instrument, rather than playing around with toy instruments.

When?

Some say that children can be ready for real lessons as soon as they're three years of age, but it may be better to wait until they're five, six, or seven, depending both on their personal development and on their instrument of choice (see pages 126–133).

The alphabet

There are various questionnaires available to assist in determining if a child is ready to start lessons. Some teachers suggest a child should be able to count to twenty-five or thirty, or to recite the alphabet to the letter H (or K, or Q…), and some specify exact minimum sizes of hands, arms, or other physical attributes as indicators of whether one is ready or not. Instructors who depend on these 'qualifiers' may help raise the average level of their students' success, but they may also steer children, talented or not, away from their musical dreams. The love for music cannot be measured in physical dimensions or academic performance.

Practicing

For children to get the most out of their lessons, they must develop good practice habits. But children below the age of seven or eight can hardly be expected to develop and maintain such a routine. Lessons for the very young are mostly about having fun and developing a love for music, rather than about steady progress and musical excellence.

Your input

Committing your child to serious music study at a very

young age requires that you be actively involved. You will usually need to be present when they practice, for example, and various early childhood music programs not only require you to attend lessons, but continue lessons at home as a 'home teacher.' There's more on this on page 25.

Reading music

Children can learn to read music around the same time they're ready to learn to read. There are all kinds of interactive games that can help your child read music in an easy, playful way. Children don't learn to read music before they're able to learn to read English; music programs for young kids teach by rote.

Singing in tune

Most children are able to sing in tune around the age six or seven. Also by that time, most can keep a basic beat, clapping their hands or dancing in time with the music: They have achieved basic musical competence. With a natural talent and enough support, some children can accomplish this much earlier. Six or seven-year-olds may also be able to figure out how to play a familiar melody on a piano or other keyboard instrument. Playing around with these and other instruments can inspire their first compositions.

Fractional instruments

The choice of instruments for children below the age of six or seven is usually limited to *orchestral strings* (available in various small, so-called *fractional* sizes; see page 105), piano or keyboard, perhaps guitar, and percussion. When they turn six or seven, they can choose from a larger (and still growing!) number of *downsized* instruments. Examples can be found on pages 126–133.

All instruments

As children get a little older, having had the opportunity to listen to various styles of music, they will become more adept at actively distinguishing the sounds and characters of the wide variety of instruments available, which will help them to decide on an instrument. Most ten to twelve-year-olds can physically handle most 'adult-sized' instruments.

Teeth

Whether or not children who either wear braces or do not have their adult teeth yet should play *wind instruments* (which exert pressure on the teeth) is still under a lot of debate — even though numerous kids have proven that it can be done. There's more on this sensitive subject on pages 51–55.

Early teens

The early teens are a time of many changes. Children who started playing at an earlier age may become more serious about their musical activities during these years — whether as a means of self-expression and self-exploration, to have fun, to make friends, to gain respect and increase self-esteem, or for any other reason. Some teens express an interest in playing an instrument for the first time in their lives. They may pick up a bass guitar to join friends in a garage band right away, or devote themselves to a lot of serious practice on the double bass so they can join the school orchestra — or anything in between.

Dropping out

Unfortunately, the early teen years can be a period of time when many children quit their musical activities for a wide variety of reasons. Because children of this age begin to discover and develop their personal and musical identities, they may discover that they actually dislike the music or the instrument they initially chose — or they just want to do things differently than you or their teachers suggest. (Remember?)

Changes

The step from elementary school to junior high brings along a lot of other changes: new friends, single-subject teachers (rather than one familiar face in front of the classroom), academic pressure and related responsibilities, and so on. Likewise, all kinds of physical changes present themselves, from pimples to the mutation of boy's voices (which definitely affects their singing). This is also the time when many kids get braces (which can hinder trumpeters, clarinetists and other wind instrument players; see page 53–55). Also, music teachers may be more demanding toward students of this age, which may spoil your child's pleasure in taking lessons. All these changes together are enough to make many children want to stop the things they previously enjoyed.

Simple?

Nevertheless, proper guidance and sufficient patience may be all you need to do to encourage your children to continue their musical studies. This may be as simple as allowing them to switch from clarinet to saxophone (or vice versa...), or to support their use of a computer as a musical tool in lieu of a traditional musical instrument. And hard as it may be, you might just have to accept their present lack of interest in music, and hope that they'll return to their instrument (or a different one) in the future. This may not happen until they leave the house, but even so, you can be happy that their early musical education paid off in the long run.

LEARNING STYLES

People pick up and process information in different ways. While observing children as they grow up, you'll notice their different learning styles and modes of development. Guiding your child's musical education may become easier if you know a little about these styles.

Touch and eat

Babies explore things by touching them (tactile learning) and by putting them in their mouths (gustatory learning). These evolve into a mixture of three main learning styles: visual, auditory and physical.

- Visual – learning by reading, via images, or through other visuals (visual learners prefer a map to a verbal explanation).
- Auditory – learning by listening — to verbal communication or even music (auditory learners prefer a lecture to reading a textbook).
- Physical – learning by physically doing things (true physical learners can hardly sit still for more than five minutes and cannot talk without using their hands).

All three

Learning to play an instrument often requires elements

from all three learning styles. You learn physically by actually operating the instrument; you need to use your auditory skills to hear yourself and your fellow musicians play, to understand your teacher, and to learn from hearing other musicians perform; and the visual element comes into play when you need to read music, or — on a guitar, for example — to see where you put your fingers.

Visual learners

Typical visual learners may get lost if you take away their sheet music or lyric sheet: Visual input is crucial to them. At the same time, they may easily pick up all kinds of playing tips and techniques from watching educational music DVDs or similar media. They're not very likely to become star improvisers. Visual learners may prefer instruments on which they can watch what they're doing — the positions of the left hand on a guitar neck, or the positions of the fingers on a keyboard. They're less likely to choose a brass instrument, for example, because it doesn't provide visual feedback. In today's society, visual learning is the prevailing learning style: Most information is offered either in print, on TV, or through the Internet.

Auditory learners

Children who easily memorize the lyrics of the songs you sing to them are probably auditory learners. Although probably not very motivated to learn to read music, auditory learners possess a particularly strong musical instinct (case in point, the exceptionally talented kids who can play every song they've heard just once). Learning to read music can be postponed for strong auditory learners, perhaps holding off until they're intellectually ready, rather than forcing it upon them too early. And yes, there are many great non-classical musicians and enthusiastic amateurs who never learned to read.

Physical learners

True physical learners tend to become drummers rather than flutists (but there are extremely sweet drummers and rowdy flute players too), lead singers rather than choir boys or girls, and they're usually more at home in a marching band than in a string quartet. They like action, and instead of waiting for an explanation or watching an educational DVD, they'd rather pick up the instrument and give it a go. They're probably the ones who like to maintain, adjust, and fix (or ruin, at first…) their own instruments too. Physical learners are also known as bodily-kinesthetic or tactual-kinesthetic (T-K, K-T) learners.

One missing
People almost always possess a combination of the above learning styles, but one usually prevails. If blind or deaf, one main learning mode is missing. Still, there are many wonderful blind and even deaf professional musicians, as well as numerous sensory-impaired amateurs who love playing music.

More learning styles
There are many more ways to distinguish one learner from another. Some examples:
- Physical learners are often **active learners**. They prefer to try things out rather than think of a plan beforehand, which is what a reflective learner would do.
- **Social (interpersonal) learners** tend to enjoy their group lessons and playing in a band more than their solitary practicing sessions, while **solitary (intrapersonal) learners** will often choose an instrument (piano or other keyboard instrument, guitar) that allows them to play by themselves.
- A **sequential learner** prefers new material to be presented in a step-by-step fashion, and will be confused by a 'global' teacher who jumps from point to point without any apparent order. Likewise, those who prefer details will not as easily comprehend a teacher who presents a big picture perspective.
- **Graphomotoric learners** need to write things down to memorize them; this style can be applied to music too.
- **Intuitive learners** like the challenge of trying something new on their own, and they're not afraid to fail and try again. Non-intuitive or sensing learners prefer step-by-step guidance and support, avoiding surprises and experiments. Likewise, there are bandleaders who fire you if you make a mistake (non-intuitive), and those who fire you when you don't (intuitive) — each type has different interpretations of what it means to give your all.

Yourself

Are you finding it difficult to define your child's learning style? Start by observing your own learning style. How do you like information to be presented? For example, do you prefer to get directions from a map or from written or spoken directions? Once you're more familiar with your own learning style, you should begin to better recognize the patterns and preferences of your child.

3. LEARNING TO PLAY

Is it hard to learn to play an instrument? No, not really. Almost anyone can do it, and almost anyone can play a number of easy pieces within a few weeks or months. On the other hand... Yes, learning to play an instrument can be a daunting task. That is if you don't do it right, or if you aim for the very highest level before you're ready. This chapter tells you everything you should know about learning to play: from early childhood programs to finding the right teacher for your child, and the differences between private and group lessons to what lessons cost. Tips on how to provide children with some basic musical education at home — even if you don't play yourself!— are also included.

Playing the piano is no more than hitting the right keys at the right time, you could say. But it's also using your ten fingers to touch an infinite combination of no less than eighty-eight keys, while your two feet control three pedals. At the very same time you also have to listen to what you play (do I play the right notes in the right order at the right tempo and the right volume?), and possibly to the sound of fellow musicians, keeping one eye at the conductor and the other on your sheet music. That makes playing the piano sound fairly complex. Still, we (and our children) can do learn to do it, just like we learn to drive cars, play computer games, and all kinds of other activities as complex as playing the piano.

Building a tower
Imagine being out in a field where lots of rocks are laying

around, and you feel like building a tower out of them. At first, you make quick progress. Stones of all sizes are within easy reach, and piling up the first few feet is quickly done. Instant gratification! But the higher the tower gets, the harder things become and the slower they go. You have to climb all the way up to position new stones, and all the way down to get new building blocks — and you have to carry them all the way up, one by one. The higher the tower becomes, the more time and energy this takes, and the harder it will be to balance things. But it's good that your tower gets higher too, because you need its height to see where to find the new rocks that help you get to the next level.

Similar

Learning to play an instrument is quite similar. The first lessons are often very rewarding. Everything is new and exciting, and within weeks, children are likely to be able to play a song all by themselves. But as time goes by, learning an instrument turns out to be a process that gives its gratification in the long term. You actually have to put in quite a lot of work before you move on to the next level of musicianship. There are long periods when progress seems slow or non-existent, and these are the times when it can be really hard to keep on practicing. Why should you, when nothing happens? Truth is that things *do* happen, but very, very gradually, and they may take a long while to show. Knowing a bit about this process can help you guide your child through these periods.

No progress, still fun

While to many musicians, progress, at any level, is essential to maintaining an interest in making music, millions of people enjoy playing at the same level for years and years. No towers to build, no stones to get; just have fun at the level where you are at. Children can reach such a level within a few years of lessons (or even sooner) on any instrument.

Talent?

Some children can sing in tune at a very young age, implying they have a good ear for pitch. Others keep a steady beat early on, which suggests a good sense of rhythm.

However, being talented in any musical way doesn't mean a child has the desire to learn an instrument. He or she may prefer to dance, or write, for example, or play ball... Conversely, many children who initially sounded horrible on the instruments they first tried, and acquired their basic musical competencies later in their childhood, have grown into successful professional musicians.

The bottom line? The talent or aptitude you may or may not spot in your children isn't that important. Don't let an apparent lack of it keep you from bringing music in their lives, and do not force your talented ones in directions they may not want to go in. First of all, let them have fun playing music.

WHAT YOU CAN DO YOURSELF

Children learn many basic skills in life by observing and imitating their parents. So why not include music? There are many things you can do to foster your child's musical development, and you don't need to be able to play yourself to do so.

Sing

Singing to and with children is an easy, fun, and very effective way to educate them musically, and it's probably good for their verbal development as well. No matter how many different songs you present, be aware that your child will probably want you to repeat their favorite song again and again. This is basically their first way to practice.

Anything

Your child will learn all kinds of songs in special music programs, but also in school. You can also sing the same old folk songs you grew up with; the good ones never seem to die.

Still need more? There are numerous books with children's songs, either with or without sheet music. To find out what a new song should sound like, all you need is the ability to play the melody on a home keyboard with a single finger, which is something you can probably learn in a matter of weeks. Alternatively, there are CDs that provide you with professional accompaniment of numerous children's songs. All you and your child have to do is sing along. If you know the melody of a song, but can't remember all of the lyrics, simply search for the title on the Internet, or visit one of the available special Websites (see page 187–188). Tip: Learning the guitar to a point where you can accompany your children's songs isn't very hard either, and both acoustic guitars and home keyboards are affordable, yet valuable, investments.

Improvise

You can also make up songs yourself, singing about what you're having for dinner, or how fine your baby looks, or anything else that comes to mind. Use a familiar melody, or make one up yourself; there are no conditions other than having fun. Older children can be inspired to make up their own songs too.

Call and response

Try call and response with your children. You sing one or two lines, and they sing their response back to you, or you inspire them to repeat what you sang. With infants, try and see what happens if you respond to your baby's sounds by making those sounds back. It works!

Odd?

With most children's songs you know, you can count along in two (1, 2; 1, 2), three (1, 2, 3; e.g., "My Bonnie Lies Over the Ocean") or four. These so-called *duple*, *triple*, and *quadruple meters* are very common in Western music. Some music programs for children also use songs from other cultures — songs where you count in 5 or 7, for example. Difficult? For us, maybe, but children pick up such 'odd' meters very easily, as do the children of such cultures where these meters are anything but odd.

Action songs

Songs that invite children to move or dance, such as "Itsy Bitsy Spider" or "Head, Shoulders, Knees, and Toes," are very helpful for a child's rhythmical development. You can simply turn any song into a so-called 'action' song by clapping and tapping along with the beat, persuading your child to join you, or — when they're still too young — clap their hands for them. Such activities teach them how to keep a beat and helps to develop their motor skills.

Dance
Dancing has a similar effect; dance to the music (any music, really) with your baby in your arms, or dance with your child as soon as they can walk. You don't need to be a good dancer. Just move to the music. That's all there is to it.

Toy instruments
Get your child toy instruments. There is a wide range of child-safe, child-proof, and affordable musical toys available, ranging from pull-along animals that produce all kinds of sounds, to toy pianos, guitars, whistles, and so on. Toy percussion instruments (frame drums, bells, shakers, tambourines) are the most accessible. Simply hitting them will do.

Play music
Play CDs or music radio stations at home rather than having the TV on 24/24. This will get children acquainted with and interested in music, and it will help their musical development through a process called *osmosis*: They absorb and learn about music without even knowing it.

All styles
There's absolutely no need to play children's songs only (you may find that unbearable after a while). Rather expose them to a variety of musical styles (and you may discover new horizons for yourself too). Play them classical music, jazz, reggae, pop, soul, country, music from other cultures, and everything else that you think sounds good. There's also a lot of special age-appropriate music around that may please you as much as them. When children get a little older, you may want to ask them which styles of music they like best, and what it is they like about those styles. This helps to make them more aware of what they're listening to.

Instrumental music
As children tend to focus on a song's lyrics rather than the melody and rhythm, it's good to also play them instrumental music, such as most types of classical music or jazz. Music programs for young children often include age-appropriate instrumental music.

Repetition

Children may be very explicit regarding which type of music or which songs they like best. Allowing them to listen to certain songs time after time is much like the repetition of practice. Children who have their own audio player (CD, MP3, etc.) can select their own songs from the music you provide for them. Various companies make special players for kids. Some even include a microphone so your young one can sing along.

TV, CD, radio?

There are TV stations that broadcast only music, but getting your musical exposure from the TV is definitely a different experience than playing CDs, or listening to radio stations. TV's visual images can actually distract children from both the music and from engaging in concurrent activities such as playing, reading, or cleaning up their rooms. Plus, music TV stations generally play primarily pop music, whereas CDs and radio offer a wide variety of styles to choose from.

Tip: Borrow CDs in your local public library so you can find out what you and your child like without spending a fortune buying albums.

Learning by listening

If you play an instrument, listening to music is an essential way to improve your own playing. As children get older, they will definitely learn a lot (how to produce a great sound on the instrument, how to interpret and perform the music, and so on) by listening to others play — especially live!.

Stay tuned

Once into their teens, children often develop new musical preferences — and just as often they grow to like a style of music that you don't like or understand (possibly the same way your parents felt about the music you liked when you were that age). Still, try to stay connected: listen along with them or sit and watch their favorite clips on TV with them (if they let you).

Tip: Some albums feature a "Parental Advisory: Explicit Content" sticker. The use of this advisory is voluntary; know what your children are listening to.

Concerts

If you want your children to get the most out of listening to music, take them to concerts. Live concerts literally add life to the music, and watching people perform is different from simply listening to music on your home stereo. Also, taking you children to concerts teaches them to correlate the various sounds they hear to the specific instruments being used.

Tips

- A benefit to most **outdoor concerts** is that, if your child seems bored, you can simply leave before they're over.
- Look for special **music events for children**, as organized by various symphony orchestras and other organizations.
- Attending concerts can be an expensive activity, but there may be more **free or affordable concerts** in your area than you think — such as college or high school bands, local church performances, and public festivals and events. Local newspapers are a good source for this information.

EARLY CHILDHOOD MUSIC PROGRAMS

There are all kinds of music classes available for the very youngest children. They're often referred to as *early childhood music programs*, *music education programs*, or *music readiness programs*.

Fun

Most of these programs are not geared towards having your child learn to play an instrument. They just get children actively involved with music in many different ways, from singing and playing musical games to moving to music and playing a variety of children's instruments, all in a very playful way. Some organizations also offer these classes for children up to ten years of age or older. Other programs offer subjects like *ear training* and ensemble playing, providing more of a solid foundation for further musical education.

Different groups

There are a number of different age ranges that these programs appeal to: some may offer classes for children from zero to eighteen months and eighteen months to three years; others have classes for zero to four-year-olds and four to seven-year-olds, for example. These age groupings are less relevant than the program's content, its underlying philosophy, and, most importantly, the people in charge. Your child should feel at ease with them, and they should be able to provide your child with a lot of fun — and music. Tip: Programs for the very young often invite or even require you to participate in the group's activities.

Music programs

Some of the better known, internationally available general music programs are Music Together, Kindermusik, and Music for Young Children. Two other names you are bound to come across are Orff Schulwerk and the Kodaly Method; many music teachers that work with young children use elements of either or both of these methodologies.

More sources

To search the Internet for these and other programs and methods, type in the terms listed above (music education program, etc.), combined with your area code or city name. Alternatively, you may check with your local recreation and community service center, or with a community music school, for instance.

Instrument-based programs

There are also instrument-based programs. The Suzuki Method, one of the best known programs, is used to teach violin, viola, cello, piano, and guitar to very young children. Parents join their children in these classes (parents also get to play the instruments themselves), and have an active role in teaching them. Children are taught to play pretty much the same way they learn to talk. Reading music is taught only after students have learned to play, just like you learn to read only once you have learned to speak. Tip: Some teens and adults prefer learning this way, too — and such courses are available. Opponents of this teaching method argue that learning to read may be difficult after learning to play because it slows the learning process down. (And why would you need to read if you can readily pick up new songs by ear?)

Costs

Exact prices for music readiness and early childhood programs depend on the type of program, as well as on where you live. In large cities, things may be more expensive than in rural areas, and prices can vary per state or country as well. Most programs cost between some forty to eighty dollars a month, based on one lesson per week.

SCHOOL MUSIC PROGRAMS

Schools differ widely in the music programs they offer, and some have even eliminated them altogether. This section offers an overview of what you may be able to expect from school programs, and offers information on what you can do if your child's school has few or no music resources.

Elementary school

Elementary schools may offer the following classes, either taught by a classroom teacher, or preferably, a certified music teacher.

- Music exploratory programs, which can include anything from singing and dancing to an introduction to composers, musical styles and instruments, music appreciation, and playing classroom instruments.
- Violin and other string instruments lessons. Some schools offer these programs as early as kindergarten.
- Wind instrument lessons.
- Recorder lessons — typically starting anywhere from 3rd to 5th grade.
- Band and/or orchestra — usually starting in 5th or 6th grade.
- Chorus.

Middle and (junior) high schools

Many middle and (junior) high schools offer both band and orchestra. 'Band' refers to a concert band or wind band, two of the many names for a large ensemble that features a variety of wind and percussion instruments. Most school orchestras are comprised of orchestral string instruments only. (These and all other types of ensembles are explained in Chapter 8.) Separate music theory and music appreciation lessons may be available as well.

Schools that offer guitar and keyboard or piano classes are great for kids who are not interested in playing traditional band and orchestral instruments. Some schools also provide computers and music software, so students can learn to digitally compose and produce music. (There are even elementary schools that teach third graders composition this way!)

High school

High schools often have a variety of band programs — a concert or symphonic band, a marching band, a jazz band, a pep band, perhaps even a mariachi band, or other types of bands. There are usually one or more choirs as well. Ideally, instrument and/or choral instruction is available for both beginners and advanced players.

College and university

Colleges and universities may have even more ensembles to choose from — especially if there's a faculty of music, of course — ranging from percussion ensembles and flute choirs to brass quintets and new music ensembles.

Ensembles may or may not be open to all qualified students; some are audition-based, but some require that the student be a music major.

A professional career

If your child is considering music as a profession, consult their high school music teacher, band director, and guidance counselor about the possibilities for further education.

Professional education is available at a wide range of public and private universities, colleges, and a few independent conservatories or schools of music.

In addition, there are institutes that offer professional, applied music education in various contemporary styles (such as rock and jazz for electric guitarists, bassists, drummers, keyboardists, etc.), as well as audio engineering, music business, songwriting, and other music-related areas.

Various examination boards offer diplomas for professional teachers and performers too (see page 58). Tip: A career in music doesn't mean a career as a musician per se. There are dozens of other musical careers, ranging from artist manager, film music editor, booking agent, composer or songwriter, and music business attorney to instrument maker, music librarian, producer, publisher, sound engineer, music critic, and so on.

Checklist

Before choosing a school, consider the information on the previous pages as well as the following list.

- Schools differ in **how much time** is available for music instruction, rehearsals, and other musical activities. Some school bands rehearse no more than once a week; others play every other day.
- Have a look at the school's **auditorium** and music class-rooms.
- What about the **quality and condition** of the school's instruments?
- Do music classes and rehearsals take place **during the day**, preferably right before or after school hours?
- Is **individual** or **small group** instruction available?
- Are there **specialized** music teachers on staff?
- Visit **school concerts**, or check out music contests sponsored by the school district. One of the best ways to judge a school's music education program is to see and hear its students play.

Pull-out lessons

Instrument instruction is often held at the same time as other class periods, requiring that the student occasionally pull out of one class to attend the instruction session. Research suggests, however, that pull-out instruction sessions do not decrease a student's academic performance; on the contrary, music students consistently score higher on their SATs and ACTs. Nonetheless, if your child's academic performance is suffering because of pull-outs, try to arrange a rotating instruction schedule that prevents him or her from being pulled out of the same class each week.

Parent-teacher association

If you want to be actively involved in the school's music program, consider joining a parent-teacher association or a parents-for-music organization. Such groups have committees that organize fund raisers (raising money for instruments, uniforms, and equipment), escort trips to performances, maintain uniforms, promote the band, and so on.

NO MUSIC?

When school budgets are cut, fine arts programs are often the first to suffer. If your child's school does not provide music instruction as an integral part of the curriculum, you will have to take care of this part of your child's education by seeking private or group lessons elsewhere (see pages 30–34). This is not a bad solution per se: In many (European and other) countries around the world, school music instruction has always been limited to a maximum of one or two hours of music appreciation lessons a week. Instrument lessons, band, orchestra, and other musical activities are simply not considered part of the school curriculum, and are considered to be the parents' responsibility.

Music advocacy

Some schools manage to keep music programs alive regardless of budget cuts; others just cannot. As a parent, you can try to re-install music as an integral part of your child's school education: You can become a music education advocate and present the case for music in the schools to the school decision-makers. Various organizations provide you with all the information, materials, and tools necessary to prepare you to become actively involved (see Music advocacy, page 187).

Grants and instruments

There are organizations and programs that offer help by providing free music classes to elementary schools, or they present grants so schools for the hiring of music teachers or the purchase of instruments. Some examples are listed on pages 189–190.

Music clubs

High school students can also take things in their own hands and start a music club, for example. Most school faculties will support such initiatives. The current teaching staff may have someone willing to act as music director. A local music store might offer a 'club discount' to members who buy or rent their gear exclusively from them. And if there's a music college in the vicinity, its students may be willing to teach the members of the club at reduced rates.

No teachers

Reduced funding is not the only reason that schools cut or decrease musical activities; in some cases, there are no qualified teachers available. One solution may be to invite undergraduate college students to teach elementary and middle school students, or to involve them and existing teachers in the many special programs available aimed at cultivating and developing qualified teachers.

HOME-SCHOOL MUSIC PROGRAMS

Some one to two million US students are home schooled, and this number is growing. If you want to enroll your home-schooled child in music lessons, look for a home-school music program in your area, either by checking the Internet or contacting your local home-school support association. Such programs usually offer music theory and music appreciation classes as well as private and group instrumental lessons.

Yourself

Home-school music programs can be initiated by a music store, for example, or by a group of home-schooling parents. If you want to set up such a program, contact local music stores, churches, and educational institutions, and ask for their willingness to provide discounts, special rental programs, rehearsal rooms, instruments, instruction, knowledge, and experience. Many successful programs have been launched this way. If funding is a problem, solicit music majors or retired music teachers who may be willing to teach or direct a band or orchestra.

INDEPENDENT INSTRUMENT LESSONS

If your children are serious about learning to play an instrument — or if you think this is an essential element of their education — their school instruction should probably be augmented with independent instrument lessons by a private teacher or community music school. Some middle schools and high schools have specialized music teachers who also give private lessons.

Special instruments
Oboe, bassoon, and French horn are often considered 'difficult' instruments to learn, and students who play them typically require additional private lessons. Without the extra instruction, students of these instruments often find it hard to keep up to speed with fellow student clarinetists, violinists, or trumpeters. That said, in the end every student will benefit from one-on-one instruction, and there's no one instrument harder than any other instrument (as discussed on page 134–136).

Too much
Talented kids need private lessons to keep them interested and to ensure that their progress is not hampered by slower classmates. For slower students, private lessons can help them keep up with the rest of the band. However, taking both private and school music instruction can be too much of a good thing for some children, making them want to quit. If that happens, it's better to choose between the two and drop the other one, rather than risk having your child miss out on a music education. Less can be more.

Preferred instrument
In school music programs, children don't always get to decide which instrument they're going to play. If your child wants to play the trumpet, enroll him or her in private lessons before the school music program starts. Already having experience in the instrument of their choice should help to ensure that your child will be assigned that instrument in the school program.

Late starters
For children who start their musical education much later, say in high school, private lessons can usually get them ready to join the school band in a matter of months.

GROUP LESSONS OR PRIVATE INSTRUCTION?
If you and your child have decided to go for additional instrument lessons, you may have to choose between small-group lessons and private instruction.

Group lessons? Yes!

While older and more advanced students will usually benefit most from private instruction, there are many things to be said for group lessons. Group lessons:

- Can be **more fun**, as most children love to do things together.
- Teach your child to be comfortable playing when **others** — besides the teacher or parents — **are listening**.
- Show children that they're **not the only ones** who make mistakes.
- Allow children to learn **from and with their peers**;
- Teach them to receive and provide **feedback**.
- **Save money**, as they're cheaper than individual lessons. (More on lesson prices on pages 35–36.)

Effective group lessons

For effective group lessons, the group should not be too large (usually three to four students; beginner groups in the early stages may be larger) and the lessons should be sufficiently long: half an hour at least. The teacher needs to be aware that the more gifted, more advanced or harder-working students may be slowed down by the group, and vice versa.

In a good, well-led group, students can even advance faster then they might in individual lessons. The fact that they need to perform for and with others probably plays a role in this: The group provides an element of competition, which can be beneficial — no one wants to stay behind.

Group lessons? No!

There are things to be said against group lessons too, of course. First of all, children do not learn and progress at the same speed. In a group, it is hard or even impossible to customize the lessons for each child and to adapt things to the individual needs of the children.

Also, there will usually be less undivided attention paid on developing the many elements that make for good musicians. There are so many things students can do wrong, that it seems impossible to get more than one student to do everything right at the same time: the right notes, proper dynamics, good posture, breathing correctly, the right technique, accurate fingering…

Your child

If your child doesn't seem to do well in a group, consider switching groups if possible, or opt for individual instruction. Solitary learners (see page 16) will likely be unhappy in a group, of course, and so will children who have problems handling negative feedback in front of others. Yet, with a good teacher, they may learn how to deal with this.

Private lessons

As children progress and get older, a one-on-one learning situation is usually preferred by both students and teachers. Some students are ready to switch from group to individual lessons after a couple of months; others do well in group lessons for a couple of years. This depends on the student, the group, the teacher, and possibly on the instrument as well. In the end, the personal attention of a private teacher is invaluable, and so is the fact that the lessons can be tailored to the individual needs of the student. Besides, there are no other students that may slow you down or force you to go faster than you can. What one considers an incentive may kill someone else's enthusiasm.

Both

Teachers may also combine group and individual lessons. Some teachers may offer both group and private lessons every week; others have students take an occasional private lesson to work on specific weak or strong points (and even a single lesson could result in remarkable progress). In addition to private lessons, some offer group lessons for general subjects such as music theory, or ear training. Another option is to add short individual lessons to each group lesson (e.g., student #1 before the lesson, student #2 after the lesson, student #3 before the lesson the following week, and so on).

Family

A tip: Some teachers and schools offer heterogeneous instrumental classes, where students play a variety of instruments of the same family. The best known example would be a string class, with a mixture of violin, viola, cello and double bass students. Such settings resemble an orchestral situation, and the ensemble may soon produce a fuller, more pleasing sound than a group of violin players only. Other experts, however, really disapprove of the idea of violinists teaching cello (and so on), stressing the differences rather than the similarities of these instruments — even for beginning students.

Vocal lessons
Individual vocal lessons usually aren't suggested before the age of ten, and many teachers don't accept students until they're twelve or older. Younger children usually learn singing in a group setting such as a children's choir or the school choir.

HOME STUDIOS AND MUSIC SCHOOLS
Many private instrumental and vocal teachers work by themselves, either from their home studio or out of a rented space in a local music store. Others may have formed a teacher's collective, and still others are employed by community music schools.

At home
Teachers with home teaching studios can be very flexible when it comes to scheduling and rescheduling lessons, for example, and you may be able to start lessons at any time of the year. Taking lessons in the comfort and privacy of a teacher's home may ease your child's anxiety, too. Home studio teachers are often completely independent. Others may be affiliated with organizations that provide structured music programs and support (such as training, educational materials, and advertising) for the teacher.

Music schools
A music school can be anything from an informal group of non-associated teachers who just happen to be renting space in the same building, to an officially sanctioned educational establishment with a clear philosophy, a wide variety of curricula, and a number of carefully selected, qualified teachers. Next to regular lessons, music schools may offer all kinds of extras such as:
• Ensembles (orchestra, band, jazz bands, rock bands, choirs, etc.) and school concerts.

- Band coaching.
- Extra classes (ear training, music appreciation, etc.).
- Master classes (taught by invited professionals and experts).
- Workshops (for specific instruments, ensembles, styles of music, etc.).
- A recording studio and/or an auditorium.
- Programs for all ages, from early childhood to teens to adults.

Community music schools

Community music schools are non-profit organizations that enroll students of all levels, are staffed with qualified teachers available at affordable rates, and usually have financial aid options available for low-income families. Community schools of the arts (see page 188) also provide dance, theater, media arts, and other classes.

LESSON TIMES AND FEES

How long do lessons last, and what do private lessons cost?

Half an hour

It is quite hard to make for an effective lesson in less than twenty minutes. Even for piano students (who don't need to unpack and tune their instrument), this is really short. Most private lessons last for half an hour.

Advanced players usually benefit from longer lessons, up to an hour or more.

Twice a week

Half an hour can be too much for a young child's attention span. If so, you may consider two short lessons per week (if your situation and the teacher of your choice allow this), with the added benefit that your child doesn't need to bridge an entire week between lessons. Conversely, older students may be better off with a longer lesson every two weeks.

Fees for private lessons

Prices for private lessons typically range from twenty to fifty dollars for one half-hour lesson on a weekly basis. The exact fee varies primarily according to where you live (cities are typically more expensive than rural areas) and the teacher's experience and qualifications. Low prices can be very attractive; but be sure you consider how qualified and effective a ten-dollar-an-hour music teacher may actually be.

A little extra

Many private teachers make house calls. In addition to the lesson, they may charge for mileage and travel time. Also, to save themselves from traveling more hours than they're actually teaching, they'll often state a maximum distance they're willing to travel. Be sure you're aware of these factors before choosing this option.

A little less

You may get a discount if you purchase a number of lessons at once, and teachers and music schools may offer a family plan (charging less for your second or third child). Also, some teachers are willing to negotiate their exact fee depending on your financial situation, or they may have sliding-scale or low-income policies.

Save money

Some other ways to save money on music lessons?

- Go to a **non-profit** community music school, or inquire if the school's music teacher also teaches privately.
- Find out if there are **music majors** in your area who are willing to teach (although an inexperienced teacher may not be the best choice for your child, even if it's cost-effective).
- Go for **group lessons** rather than private lessons (group lessons may cost as little as fifteen dollars for a weekly fifty minute lesson).
- See if it's possible to change from weekly to **biweekly lessons** (though this is generally not advisable for younger students).
- Find out if there are s**cholarships or other funding** available from local service organizations, arts councils, or special programs. Band directors, music teachers, and teachers' associations and related organizations (see pages 186–189) should be able to advise you on where to find information. Some schools have scholarships available for private lessons.

TEACHERS

The following sections offer helpful hints on how to find and assess a teacher, as well as notes on different teaching styles.

A side job?

Finding the right teacher for your children is crucial. Don't simply settle for the one next door just because they charge low fees and offer instructions on umpteen different instruments. Teaching music is about making children enjoy playing and practicing, and instilling a love for music that could last a lifetime. Such a task requires a good, dedicated teacher.

Seeking a teacher

There are many ways to seek a teacher or a music school in your vicinity.

- Ask **friends**, **family**, and **neighbors**.
- Consult with **school music teachers**; they often maintain lists of qualified private teachers.
- High school **music directors**, church music directors, the local orchestra (whose members often teach too), and the music department at your local college can also be good sources.
- **Music stores** may have teachers on staff. If not, they can refer you to a number of teachers in the area.
- Contact your state's **music teachers association** (search for 'music teachers association' and the name of your state on the Internet), art councils, or your local recreation and community services department.
- A number of **special-interest Websites** can help you find a teacher in your area. These databases usually offer a limited number of teachers only. Please see page 189 for examples.
- Using a general **search engine** (search for "piano teacher" and "Long Beach" for example) can work, but such search strings may also produce irrelevant hits.
- Check classified ads in music magazines and local newspapers
- Visit the **public library**, or contact the local chamber of commerce.
- Consult the *Yellow Pages* or similar sources.

GOOD TEACHERS

Anyone can refer to themselves as a music teacher. So how do you find a good one?

Rapport

A good teacher is genuinely interested in making your child enjoy music to the fullest, developing your child's art habit, and turning music into an inherent — and entertaining, relaxing, stimulating, exciting — part of his or her life. To do so, a teacher must be able to establish a good rapport with your child. Children should feel perfectly safe and at ease with their teachers.

It's critical that teachers are not only able to convey music in a way that children understand, but that they also incite an enthusiasm and hunger for music. They also need to be able to make the children feel good about their musical performance, even at times when there's little or no progress. A private instrumental or vocal teacher is often your child's only one-on-one tutor (!) so the quality of their relationship really counts. More often than not, these teachers become important role models for your offspring.

Long-term

The above implies that students preferably stay with the same private teacher for at least a couple of years. Changing teachers can slow a child's progress; kids may feel they have to start all over again, and new faces and habits may ruin carefully established musical routines. However, if a child seems to dislike, or cannot understand the instructions of, or is not inspired by his or her teacher, changing instructors might prevent your child from quitting. There's much more on this sensitive subject in Chapter 5.

Good relationship

If a good relationship with their teacher has been established, children will be able to express their musical preferences and feel that they're being taken seriously. If the rapport between the teacher and student is open and trusting, a student can simply tell his or her teacher that they'll have less time for practice next week because of a school project, for example, without upsetting anyone.

Learning styles

Good teachers know how to work with children with different learning styles and preferences. They can offer clearly structured lessons for those who need them, and offer other students more freedom and room for improvisation. They can explain things in either a step-by-step format or in the big-picture, depending on the student's needs. Even so, keep in mind that student-teacher relationship are unique and personal: a teacher who does wonders with your first-born may not get anywhere with your second child.

All of you

A good instructor not only teaches you how to play an instrument, but helps you discover how playing the instrument can make you feel better, raise your self-esteem, help you express your feelings, and so much more. In that sense, a music instructor teaches much more than the mechanics of hitting notes or strumming strings; they coach self-awareness and self-expression. Such teachers will also motivate your child to keep on playing when progress seems unnoticeable — and every musician, at every level, goes through that experience more than once (as discussed on page 19).

DIFFERENT TEACHERS

Just like all individuals, music teachers have different personalities, philosophies, methods, experiences, and ideas. Here are some random thoughts.

Answers or questions

In the old days, teachers used to tell you what to do, and that was basically it. Nowadays, most people favor teachers who pose questions rather than simply providing answers. A teacher who inspires you to discover things for yourself is often more effective than someone who gives strict directives only. It's the difference between, "Don't tighten those muscles!" and someone asking, "Can you feel what happens if you relax those muscles?" It may also be the difference between an authoritarian, demanding, no-nonsense teacher and one with exceptional communication skills who feels music should be fun rather than produce high grades. That said, the latter can be just as demanding, and 'fun' teachers scold and 'push' you to be a better player — not because they dislike you or want to be mean, but because they care and can see your potential. A teacher who says you've done well when you know you didn't can be as detrimental and unmotivating as one who is never satisfied with your performance.

A good teacher senses when you're frustrated (from playing music that is too difficult), or bored (from playing music that is unchallenging). That balance differs from student to student.

Assignments

Likewise, students can become frustrated because they get too many assignments or bored if they have too few. Students should be able to accomplish the goal of each assignment in the time between lessons. Teachers should provide their students with progress checkpoints (e.g., being able to play the first sixteen bars after two days of practice, and the first thirty-two after five), which help students measure their own small successes. These successes are great motivators.

Candy bar?

If your child wants to play the drums, anyone can teach him or her how to play a basic rock beat in a matter of days, offering instant gratification. But if children want to learn to master an instrument, rather than just learning to play a song, they'll need to be in it for the long haul. And with a good teacher, they'll enjoy most of those years. Choosing teachers, in that sense, is like deciding what to give your children for breakfast: a candy bar, or something nutritious that will serve them in the long run? This doesn't mean that learning to play songs at an early stage is a bad thing; it can get them motivated past the tedium of playing scales exclusively.

In the end, however, music lessons should probably focus on music, not just on songs. It's true that taking lessons from a teacher of rock guitar may help you become a great rock guitarist. But what if your interests shift to jazz later on? The best instructors teach you the instrument in its entirety. And even more than that, they teach music, allowing you to follow any musical path you want.

Show the other side

Students attempting perfection in their playing should perhaps not begin a new piece before conquering the first one; students less interested in flawlessness and more interested in variety may quit if a teacher keeps them honing pieces they feel they're done with. That said, a good teacher will help the perfectionist see how counter-productive too much meticulousness can be, and show the second student how rewarding it is to master a song before moving on.

Custom lessons

Student-centered teachers tailor their lessons to their students' needs, preferences, limitations, talents, learning styles, and goals. This doesn't mean that they won't ask your child to play a piece he or she doesn't like: Many children only grow to like a piece once they can play it. For *method-centered* teachers, it's not the student but the method that prevails. They often use a set program that students have to match, which provides clear-cut routes and goals, so you (and your child) always know where you stand. This method can also be an advantage when students have to switch teachers because the program simply continues as before.

Listen

Good instructors teach their students not only to play, but to actively listen to music. (As such, students not only learn to appreciate music as an art form, but become more adept at hearing wrong notes and self-correcting when practicing.) They also teach their students how to produce a good tone and how to express themselves musically (rather than just playing the correct notes at the desired tempo).

... And more

Some teachers may also incorporate into their lessons singing and movement (important primarily for younger children), music theory, ear training, improvisation and solo playing, and composition. Good teachers should also spend time on their students' posture, breathing technique, and all other elements that come into play when learning an instrument. They should also advise their students on how to plan and organize their practice sessions. See pages 81–86 for tips on this particular subject.

ASSESSING A TEACHER

Selecting the right teacher for your child often includes interviewing prospective teachers.

Who do you teach?

Many teachers accept any and all students, regardless of age, skill, or level. Others prefer to teach children exclusively. Some don't accept children under a certain age, or students who are just starting, or those who don't play well enough yet. Teachers also differ in what they demand of their students. Can children study with this teacher just for fun, or do they have to be diligent and prove their commitment and desire to learn?

Two or ten?

If you and your child are serious about learning to play an instrument, a specialized teacher — in addition to the school music teacher — will usually be the best choice. Tip: Some teachers indicate the level up to which they teach by listing their highest grade examination course taught, possibly even per instrument. See page 58–61 for more information.

Good enough

Can a cheap, used instrument in a bad state of repair be good enough to begin with? Yes, it can. But be aware that it won't likely sustain your child beyond the early stages. You may want to keep this in mind when seeking a teacher too. You wouldn't let someone who simply happens to speak English teach your child how to write, so why would you let anyone who happens to play an instrument teach your child to play? (And as for teachers who claim they can make your child a star, ask yourself why are these teachers not stars themselves…)

Qualifications

Most good, professional teachers have college, conservatory, or university credentials to support their experience with their instrument, or they have a teaching diploma from one of the recognized examination boards (see pages 58 and 188). Many are also certified by the Music Teachers National Association or a similar organization. (see page 186).

Affiliations

Most teachers are also affiliated with one or more instrument-based organizations (e.g., National Flute Association, Percussive Arts Society), state-based organizations (e.g., Florida Music Educators Association), or national organizations (e.g., American Music Center, Chamber Music America). Not all of these organizations require their members to meet certain competencies or standards.

Great musician?

One's level of musicianship doesn't say too much about how proficient at teaching one is. There are phenomenal teachers who aren't great players, and great musicians who can't teach. You and your child may be better of with a moderate musician who loves to teach, rather than a great musician who teaches to makes some extra bucks. Some parents ask a prospective teacher to play a bit to see how their child responds; This is more about style, sound, and inspiration than assessing the quality of the teacher as a musician, of course.

Special needs

Is your child a special learner? Find a teacher who knows how to deal with special needs. Such instructors are available, even though their education may not have included specific training in this area. (See pages 56–57.)

Feedback

What about feedback on your child's progress? Some teachers provide you with a weekly report; others call you every month, and some wait for you to contact them. Establish from the start the pattern of feedback that suits you, the instructor, and your child.

Recitals and competitions

Ask prospective teachers whether they hold studio recitals as an opportunity for students to perform for parents, friends, family, and fellow students. If you believe that competitions (see page 62) or examinations (see page 58) are essential to a solid music education, find out if the teacher supports this philosophy and will help prepare your child for such events. Of course this requires that the teacher be familiar with relevant organizations, exam syllabi, etc.

Studio hours
The optimum lesson time for younger children is usually before 6:00 PM or on the weekends; for teenagers, lessons are best in the early evening as well. If you want to attend your child's lessons, times may be harder to schedule. For most children, it's best to have a standard lesson time; the best situation, then, is one in which the teacher is not frequently rescheduling lessons due to other obligations.

Studio policy
Most professional teachers have a written studio policy that lists rules regarding cancellations, rescheduling, payments, and so on. Ask for a copy and carefully read it before you commit. Should you avoid teachers who don't have a written policy? This may be an indication that you're dealing with an amateur, but there are great teachers who simply prefer a more organic approach to their business.

Notebook
It's advantageous if your child has a notebook or lesson diary, in which the teacher lists weekly assignments, provides short reports on their lessons and progress, and so on. Teachers may ask you to record your child's practice times in the notebook, or to sign the weekly assignments to ensure them that you're aware of and involved in your child's education. Some teachers also have their students use the notebook to comment on the pieces they play (e.g., do they like them or not, and why; what did you find difficult?), or on how their practice sessions went.

Website
As an alternative to the paper notebook, teachers may provide their students with a Website, forum, or 'bulletin board' to be used for everything listed above, as well as for emailing additional instructions, asking and answering questions, sending reminders and other messages (lesson times, payment, etc.), providing practice tips, and so on.

Facilities

A teaching studio can be anything from a tiny cubicle in a music store to a spacious hall where an entire band could rehearse. Some have nothing but two chairs and a music stand, while others provide all the conveniences you could think of.

- Can you **park your car**, preferably off street?
- Is there a **waiting room**, and can the washroom be used?
- For students who use the house instrument (piano, drums, etc.): Does the instrument seem **in good repair** and does the equipment look professional and up to date?
- Can lessons be **recorded** on audio or video for home reference (see pages 46–47)? Tip: If your child plays a melody instrument (violin, clarinet, trumpet, etc.), it's nice if the teacher can provide accompaniment tapes that your child can play along with.
- Are **teaching materials** available (method books, etc.)?

GETTING THE MOST OUT OF LESSONS

To get the most out of lessons, an efficient practice routine is crucial. Pages 81–86 tell you everything you'd like to know on this specific subject. Here are some other tips.

Read

First of all, read the studio policy so you know when payment is due, what to do if a lesson needs to be rescheduled, or how to cancel if your child is ill and can't make it, etc. Most teachers and schools have a 24-hour cancellation policy (if you don't call at least twenty-four hours before the scheduled time, you'll have to pay for the unattended lesson). However, should something go wrong at the last minute, please call to say your child won't be there, even if the lesson has been paid for, so the teacher isn't waiting (or worrying!) needlessly. Not all teachers and schools offer make-up lessons; most that do require that make-up lessons occur within seven days of the absence.

Quitting

If your child wants to quit, most schools and teachers require you to inform them well in advance. Some schools and teachers charge you by the month (usually to be paid in advance), regardless of whether there are four or five weekly lessons in that month; and if your child quits mid-month, you'll likely forfeit the money paid in advance. Again, do read the studio policy. If there's no written policy, ask the teacher about his or her rules on these and other matters. Tip: If a teacher cancels a 'fifth' lesson, they're usually not required to make it up.

On time

If children arrive late, teachers aren't required to extend the lesson time in order to give them the full session (and there may be other students scheduled for the following hour) — so make sure your kids are on time. If there's no waiting area, try not to be there too early either.

Method books

If a teacher asks that your child obtain a method book or other materials, make sure your child has it for the next lesson. If a specific edition has been requested, don't substitute. Contact the teacher if you're having trouble finding that edition.

Additional materials

Of course, you're free to purchase additional books and materials for your child, but it's usually best to consult the teacher before you do so. Some books may be too difficult or too easy for your child at this time, or they may veer too far from the teacher's curriculum in other ways. Always inspire your children to play and to practice, but don't encourage them to do more than their teacher has asked.

The instrument

Try to ensure that your child's instrument is in good working order before every lesson, if possible. Replacing guitar strings or selecting another reed during the lesson time is a waste of valuable lesson time if these things could have been managed in advance. Likewise with tuning up: If there's a waiting area, your child may be able to unpack, assemble, and tune the instrument before the lesson starts, rather than during it.

Recording the lesson

Recording the lessons allows your child to replay everything that was said and to review their own or their teacher's playing. All you need is a basic cassette recorder with a built-in microphone. For better results, use a minidisc recorder or another digital type of recorder, preferably with a separate microphone.

Attending lessons
Some teachers will happily invite you to all your child's lessons; others prefer not to have you around. Attending your child's first two or three lessons will give you an impression of what he or she is up to, and it will give you ample time to get to know the teacher. Some parents attend the first or the last minutes of each lesson, so they are always up to date on their child's progress and assignments. Others attend every single lesson for the first half year or so. If you attend the lessons, see if the teacher is willing to let you have a go at the instrument yourself, so you can have a better understanding of your child's experience.

Be in touch
If the teacher doesn't contact you from time to time, do stay in touch yourself to learn how your child is progressing. Also, inform the teacher when your child has been unable to practice (due to sickness, school projects, or whatever), so the instructor knows what to expect from your child, and your child doesn't need to be embarrassed by not being prepared.

Summer sessions
Academic progress doesn't seem to be hindered by summer vacation, but if children don't attend music lessons for more than a couple of weeks, they will have a lot of catching up to do. So much, actually, that it may make them want to quit: It can be quite frustrating if you can't play most of the songs that you could before summer vacation started. If your child's teacher doesn't teach during the summer months, you may want to encourage your child to participate in summer sessions or a music camp. (Search the Internet for 'summer camp,' specifying the instrument, your state, and other relevant information, or ask the music teacher.)

One more
Not playing for a week or longer can negatively affect wind

instrument players more so than most other musicians. Returning to the wind instrument can readily produce sore lips and other unpleasant symptoms. The more you regularly play, the faster the effect of not playing will be noticeable. For most musicians of all instruments, playing a long session right after a long break is a bad idea, if you want to prevent blisters and painful fingers.

WITHOUT A TEACHER

Countless people around the world have learned to play without any formal training whatsoever — and that includes lots of professional and famous musicians (albeit outside of the classical world). Some instruments are better suited to self-instruction than others. Most self-taught musicians play guitar, bass guitar, drums, keyboard, or they sing. But you can learn to play any instrument without a teacher. The following section, which is mainly relevant for parents of teens, addresses this.

So why?

If children want to play an instrument but refuse to attend lessons, you may try to persuade them with some of the following:

- Why **re-invent the wheel** when there are so many people who have experience and can help you? Go once just to get started — and then feel free to go back if you get stuck or don't progress. Teachers have been trained to show you a way out of ruts and round brick walls.
- There are teachers who can help you play **the music you want to play** without forcing you to learn things you don't want to learn, whether that's music theory, scales, or whatever. (A really good teacher will probably inspire your kid toward those subjects in the end, as they will know how to impress upon them their importance.)
- If you teach yourself to play, you may end up learning things **the wrong way**. Bad habits won't get in your way as this stage, but as you progress, they may become obstacles to your becoming an excellent player. And ridding yourself of bad habits usually takes more time than getting things right from the start.
- **Teachers do much more** than simply demonstrate how to hit the right notes (you may be able to do that yourself,

after all). They also advise you on how to best utilize your strong points and how to deal with your weaknesses. And of course, they teach you to sound as good as you can.

- Lots of **famous self-taught musicians** eventually sought some training from a teacher!
- Have you ever met someone who was **sorry** that he had studied with a good teacher?

Books and DVDs

Can you learn an instrument from a book, an educational DVD or an interactive Website? Surely, you can garner much from such media. However, they can't hear what you play or watch you play, and therefore they can't provide you with feedback. In other words, they provide information but no guidance; they cannot *teach* you. The same goes for the learning tools you find on various home keyboards (e.g., built-in lights that indicate which key to play next). No matter how advanced and interactive these systems are, they can't replace a real live teacher. Also, teaching yourself alone with such media requires a lot of self-discipline, whereas having to visit a teacher each week may be a better means for keeping you going (and practicing and progressing).

What they can do

Books, DVDs, and the Internet can be very helpful, though — especially as an addition to lessons or if you've had lessons in the past. Tip: Many well-know pop, rock, Latin, and jazz artists have their own instructional DVDs from which your child can study his or her favorite artist's style and technique at their own pace (provided your child's playing level is on par with the instructional material). Beware that not all of these DVDs are of great educational value, but your child may find them inspirational.

Reading music

Teens would often rather not learn to read music, especially when their motive is to play drums, electric guitar, or bass in a garage band or a similar group. And truthfully, you can learn to play these instruments well enough to join a band much faster than you can learn to read music. Besides, as teenagers may tell you, many great songs have been composed by musicians who can't read a note, and there are countless professional musicians who don't sight-read. They're right. You can enjoy playing and even have a great musical career without reading music. So what can you tell your child?

- Learning to read music is **not difficult** at all*. Once you get the basics down (which a six-year-old can easily do, so why not you?) it's simply a matter of sticking with it; you'll get better automatically.
- Being able to read gives you **instant access to new music**. There are loads of books you can benefit from — books with great ideas for songs and solos, books with effective exercises, books in which your favorite musicians show you how they do it, and so on.
- It allows you to **play** with musicians that you have never met before. This also widens the range of gigs you can play, whether you're an amateur or a pro.
- If you can read music, you can also write it. If you get a great idea for a new song, solo, or exercise, writing it down is **easier and more reliable** than remembering it.
- You won't be lost if somebody asks you to play sixteenths instead of eighths, or when your fellow musicians speak of diminished chords or flatted sevens.
- Realize that you can **forget about all those notes** once you

Chord diagram

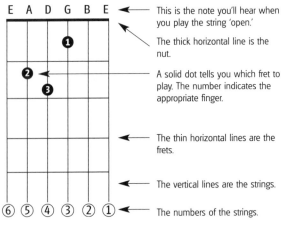

This is the note you'll hear when you play the string 'open.'

The thick horizontal line is the nut.

A solid dot tells you which fret to play. The number indicates the appropriate finger.

The thin horizontal lines are the frets.

The vertical lines are the strings.

The numbers of the strings.

Put your index finger (1) on string 3 in the first position, your middle finger (2) on string 5 in the second position, and your ring finger (3) on string 4 in the second position. This is an E-major chord.

* Tipbook Music on Paper *makes learning how to read music really easy; see page 191.*

start playing. That'll make you sound better too! (Tip: There's a section on memorizing music on pages 89–92.)

Tablature

The tablature staff represents a guitar neck. Tablature doesn't allow for precise rhythmical notation.

Chord diagrams and tablature

In addition to traditional music notation, there are various other ways to put music on paper: Guitar and keyboard chords can be represented by *chord diagrams*, guitar and bass solos can be shown in *tablature*, and similar notation systems exist for drums and other instruments. However, all of these alternatives have their limitations (e.g., tablature doesn't allow for exact rhythmic notation, and music is much more than just chords).

DENTAL AFFAIRS: THE CHANGEOVER

If your child plays a wind instrument, will braces and the changeover from baby to permanent teeth interfere with the learning process? Opinions differ. The good news is that many children actually become better musicians if they keep on playing with braces, or during their changeover. Opinions also differ when it comes to playing a wind instrument with baby teeth. For every teacher who is opposed to having children play wind instruments before they have their permanent teeth, you'll be able to find one who isn't — so the decision is basically up to you.

One-to-one

Whether it's about braces or playing a wind instrument before your child's permanent teeth have come in, one-to-one attention and personal guidance from a dedicated teacher is essential.

Better musicians?

One of the common errors children make when learning a wind instrument is applying too much pressure; and it's this pressure that causes the problems and pain associated with braces and the changeover. The solution is to simply minimize the pressure. Children who learn this have an even greater advantage, as playing with less pressure and tension makes them better musicians.

Clarinet, trumpet, flute

The most widely chosen wind instruments for younger children are the clarinet (rather than the larger saxophone), the flute, the trumpet and the cornet, and the recorder. Can children play these and other wind instruments before getting their permanent teeth? Yes, and numerous kids do and have done so without any problems whatsoever.

- To produce a pleasant tone and gain control of the **clarinet**, don't bite or 'grip' the mouthpiece. Don't use your jaw muscles (the ones you use for biting), but instead use the facial muscles surrounding the lips. After all, this instrument can be played by a person without front teeth. Can playing the clarinet push the front teeth outward? This seems to be unlikely, as this rarely even happens as a result of thumb sucking, and most toddlers spend more time sucking their thumbs than children do playing their instrument.

- The changeover can make **flute** playing a bit uncomfortable, but many children have sufficient control over their lips, which means they don't need the additional support of their front teeth.

- Things can be awkward for **trumpet and cornet** players, but a dedicated teacher can help them through this period. Problems can be prevented or reduced by selecting repertoire without high notes (e.g., the notes D5 and up, which demand extra pressure), or by adapting pieces with high notes.

- For the **recorder**, another woodwind instrument that's often played by youngsters, you use lip pressure only.

- Most kids don't start on **oboe or bassoon** before they acquire their permanent teeth, simply because these instruments are too heavy and too large for them before that time. Down-sized versions do exist, however (see pages 129–130), and they're perfectly playable without front teeth or during the changeover.

A year from now?

However, none of this means that problems won't occur, but if your child insists on a wind instrument, giving it a try is often better than telling him or her to wait for a year or two (as if they'd understand that concept anyway). Should the changeover cause more problems than your child can handle, then you might want to consider an alternative instrument for the time being, or forever. A break in a child's musical education is sometimes for good.

DENTAL AFFAIRS: BRACES

Will braces keep your child from playing a wind instrument? In most cases, no. Will the braces cause initial discomfort and take some getting used to? Yes, they will. Some children actually have to give up because of their braces — and once they stop, there's no guarantee that they'll return to it. So if your orthodontist advises that your child not play a wind instrument at all, you may want to get a second opinion (preferably from a dental expert who loves music!).

Flute? No! Yes!

While some children are advised to play the clarinet rather than the flute because of braces, others are told to play the flute rather than the clarinet — because of braces. Likewise, some say that braces should pose no problem for budding bassoon players, but there are some children who simply can't play this instrument with them. The truth is, the exact effect of braces on your child's playing depends on the combination of the type of braces, your child's physiology, your child's instrument, and his or her playing experience. Experts' opinions differ, so make the decision based on your child's situation.

The problem

With most wind instruments, braces can induce pain as the insides of the lips are pressed against the braces' hooks and wires — they can actually cut your lips. (Using a medicated mouthwash to cleanse and disinfect those tiny injuries is not a bad idea.) Luckily, your child's lips will toughen up in time. Braces will also hurt a little every time they get adjusted, and each adjustment takes some getting used to. Also, braces may cause an overabundance of saliva, which can hinder playing. But this usually gets better over time.

The solution

Always inform your orthodontist of the instrument your child plays. He or she may be able to adjust the braces accordingly so they'll cause as little problems as possible. Having an orthodontist sensitive to and experienced with such needs — perhaps one who actually plays a wind instrument — helps. A tip: Some types of braces can simply be taken out when you play. If not, there are several ways to reduce the discomfort of the braces' sharp points. These are discussed on page 55.

Flutists

One of the biggest problems for flutists is that braces may change the critical position of their lips. This alters the sound by making it a bit thin, misty, or fuzzy. Each type of braces causes a different effect, but, under the guidance of a good teacher, these effects can all be dealt with. The adjustment usually takes from a couple of days to some two weeks. Lower braces can be a bit more troublesome than upper braces, as the flute rests against the lower lip. If braces are hindering the directing of the air stream, try making the lip plate a little thicker by sticking one or more pieces of duct tape or masking tape on the lower part.

Clarinetists and saxophonists

Braces can be painful for clarinetists and saxophonists as well, and they can induce a fuzzy, airy tone at first. Adjustment often takes two weeks to a month. Braces usually hurt more as you clench your jaws more, which you shouldn't do anyway. Tip: Changing the angle of the instrument may ease the discomfort.

Brass players

For brass players, it may take longer to adjust, as they have to learn to minimize the pressure of the instrument against their lips, which will make playing high notes hard at first. If the braces really hurt, teachers may select a repertoire without high notes, or make adjustments to such sections. Using a mouthpiece with a wider rim (distributing the pressure over a larger surface) may help. Instruments with small mouthpieces (e.g., trumpet, cornet, French horn) typically cause more problems than the brass instruments with larger mouthpieces, such as trombones or baritones. Some kids do switch to another brasswind to solve the problem.

Oboists and bassoonists

For oboists and bassoonists, the discomfort of braces can be eased by using a lighter reed, which reduces the pressure on the lips. Lighter reeds will make for a thinner, more piercing sound, but that's a small price to pay. Most players will get used to their braces in two weeks or so.

Tissue, wax, and more

There are several other ways to reduce the discomfort caused by the many hooks and wires of braces:

- A readily available stopgap solution: Line the braces with **tissue**.
- Ask the orthodontist for a special **wax stick**. Rubbing the wax along the braces will cover the sharp points.
- As an alternative, there are various types of commercially available **bumper guards, caps or cushions** that cover the braces, and a system that allows you to custom-make your own brace cover. (Some names to check out: Braceguard, Morgan Bumpers, and the Jet-Tone Lip Protector.) Note that guards and covers that add too much mass to the braces may reduce the players' control over their lips.
- Tip: Tell your child to **stop practicing when it hurts**. Take things easy, and understand that progress may slow down for a while. A bit of extra personal guidance can be essential.

When they come off

Children should be prepared for another potential adjustment period when the braces come off. Sometimes the loss of braces takes more time to get used to than getting them. Tip: There are a number of special exercises that help your lips get back in shape as soon as possible. Ask your teacher for help.

CHILDREN WITH SPECIAL NEEDS

There are trumpet players who were born with a harelip, professional musicians with profound hearing loss, and severely handicapped keyboard players who press the keys with their tongue… Children that really want to play music are able to overcome pretty much any type of disability. (There's a short section on physical impairments and choosing an instrument on page 125–126.)

Hearing impairment

Children who are deaf or hearing-impaired can enjoy music by feeling the vibrations. Some can even tune their instrument via vibrations. Many of them can join the school band or orchestra, as they can rely on watching the conductor and their fellow musicians, rather than listening, to know when to stop or start. Also, there are *signing choirs* for the hearing impaired, performing everything from Broadway hits to rock songs.

Visual impairment

There are several popular artists who are blind — Stevie Wonder, Ronnie Milsap, Ray Charles. Because they can't read music, visually impaired children must learn to play by ear, memorize music, and improvise. Since classical music requires that its musicians read music, the most appropriate genres for visually impaired children to study are rock, pop, folk, jazz, or related styles.

Dyslexic children

There are various degrees of dyslexia. Given time, dyslexic children can typically learn to read music, just like they can learn to read text. There are plenty of dyslexic music teachers to prove this. *Sight-reading* (reading the notes of a piece as you play) will often be impossible, however. The note names (C, D, E, F, G, A, B) may be harder for them to read than notation (if you reverse the image of a note, as dyslexic children often do with letters, it is still the same note).

Like visually impaired children, children with severe dyslexia may be better off learning to play by ear, and studying jazz, rock, pop or similar styles rather than classical music. Tip: Reading music while listening to a performance of the piece may be very helpful.

Four times the same note–no matter how you perceive it. (Note that the first two are correct, the latter two aren't.)

Mentally challenged children

Mentally challenged children often respond very strongly to music. Numerous musical games and programs have been developed to help them connect with others, guide their social behavior, and reach their inner worlds. Likewise, autistic children can benefit from specific musical group activities. The musical performance of mentally challenged individuals often equals that of developmentally appropriate children of the same mental age, and individual instruments lessons can provide them with much joy.

Learning impaired children

Unfortunately, most music education programs don't include courses on teaching children with learning (or any other) disabilities, even though an estimated thirty to forty percent of all children fall into this category to some degree. This high percentage indicates the importance of finding a teacher who really relates to your child and brings out the best in them. Some teachers attend special courses on working with impaired children, while some simply have a natural talent for doing so.

Gifted children

Gifted children have special needs too. More often than not, they have exceptional abilities in more than one area. Should that not include music, playing in an ensemble can make a gifted child feel as though they belong to a group — moreso than they often do elsewhere. If music is one of your child's special abilities, and a musical career is being considered, it's good to know that there are special schools, accelerated classes, and specialized teachers at your child's disposal. Associations for Gifted Children will offer further information.

EXAMS AND COMPETITIONS

In many countries, music exams have been a highly valued part of every child's musical education for generations. In countries where this isn't the case, however, the quality of music education hasn't seemed to suffer. What kind of exams and grading systems are there, what are the pros and cons, and what about participating in individual competitions?

Instrument graded exams

There are various organizations that offer graded examinations on instruments. Unfortunately, there is no internationally standardized grading system, as you will see below. Some organizations may recognize certain examinations, but not others, and transfer credits are usually not offered. Websites of the following organizations can be found on page 188.

- Exams of the **Association of Royal Schools of Music** (ABRSM) can be taken in more than ninety countries. Grades 1 to 3 are for elementary players; 4 and 5 are for intermediate players, and 6–8 for advanced musicians. There's a Prep Test at a pre-Grade 1 level for the very youngest, and the ABSRM has exams for professionals as well.
- The Canadian **Royal Conservatory of Music** (RCM) has similar examinations, but their grading system is different (1, intermediate; 5–7, late intermediate; 8–10, advanced). Preparatory A and B are for beginners in their first two years. In the US, RCM examinations are offered under the name of Royal American Conservatory Examinations. The RCM has exams for a teacher's and a performer's diploma too.
- **Trinity-Guildhall** (UK) was the first international examinations board.
- In Australia and New Zealand, examinations are offered by the **Australian Music Examinations Board** (AMEB) and **Australian and New Zealand Cultural Arts Limited** (ANZCA).
- The **Yamaha** Music Education and Examination System has received international recognition in more then forty countries. Their grading system starts at Grades 13–10 for beginners; Grades 2 and 1 are their concert artist awards.
- The New York-based **NYSSMA** grades music from 1, very easy, through to 6, very difficult. A level 6+ pieces can be played by very advanced players and pros only.

- **Other organizations** use a letter system rather than figures: 'A' usually being the highest level.

What?

The exact requirements for each grade are listed in a syllabus that can be applied for through the examination board of your choice. Exams usually consist of the following parts:

- Playing one or more prepared pieces (usually to be chosen from a repertoire list of required works) and a number of scales and arpeggios.
- Sight-reading.
- Aural tests, such as identifying scales, chords, or intervals by ear.

Which grade?

There's no need to start with Grade 1. If the teacher feels your child is ready for Grade 4, he or she can usually take that exam right away. Of course, the teacher needs to be familiar with the requirements of the examination board. Tip: Exams are usually open for everyone, regardless of age and previously passed exams, and whether you have a teacher or not. It follows that you can also skip grades.

When?

What level 'Grade 4' or 'Grade 8' is, exactly, depends on the examination board, as indicated above. As a guideline, most fifteen to eighteen-year-olds are able to pass ABSRM Grade 8 and the generally equivalent RCM Grade 10, while talented kids may pass those grades when they're twelve or thirteen. Students often pass one grade per year, but you can also pass two, or you can take your next grade after two or more years of study: Exams can usually be taken throughout the year. Ideally, students take exams when they and their teachers think they're ready, and not because a certain period of time has passed or because it happens to be that time of year.

Theory

There are theory exams as well. Some boards require that you have passed, say, their Grade 5 Theory of Music before you can take Grades 6, 7, or 8 Practical on your instrument. Other boards let you take any grade without a proven knowledge of theory, as they believe that practical grades are about evaluating a performance only.

Classical only?
Not all examination boards offer non-classical grades, but some do, from jazz piano and jazz trumpet to ensemble playing.

Milestones or hurdles?
Experts often see exams as milestones that gauge a student's progress, or as essential stepping-stones in the learning process, providing students with a specific goal to focus on, thus inspiring them to practice. Knowing where you're going can definitely make you work harder. Others consider exams as hurdles in the learning process, disrupting the student's natural progress. Yet, there are students who like jumping hurdles... Here are some random thoughts on the pros and cons of taking exams.

Pros
- Taking an exam is a **reward** for having practiced diligently.
- Passing an exam often makes students **proud** of what they've achieved, inspiring them to move on.
- Taking exams provides you with helpful comments from someone **other than your teacher**.
- Passing a grade may help you get **into a band** or orchestra.
- Having a framed, graded certificate on the wall is **physical evidence** of a student's hard work.
- Many students are **challenged** by exams and love taking them.
- Exams offer a **performance opportunity**.
- A syllabus provides students and teachers with a clearly **structured educational program** so students know exactly what is expected of them.
- Exams can make or break your **confidence**.
- Exams and grades introduce an element of **competition** into the music.

Cons
- Music is about having fun and enjoying yourself, not about taking exams. Exams are **scary**.
- An exam can easily turn into a **goal in and of itself**, becoming the sole purpose of practicing rather than

something to pass by as you progress.

- Being able to perform well on an exam does not automatically mean you're able to perform well in front of **an audience**.
- Exams make students **focus too much** on required pieces (and perfect them until they're no fun to play anymore), rather than inspiring them to explore other repertoires as well.
- Many children will never get **beyond a certain level**. The obligation to take exams will confront them with their limited abilities and make them want to stop, while they could have enjoyed making music for the rest of their lives.
- If a teacher provides students with **proper feedback and encouragement**, there's no need for exams to prove they're progressing.
- Exams offer a performance opportunity — but who needs **a performance in which you can fail**?
- (Most) exams don't test how you **perform in a band** or an orchestra.
- Exams can make or break your **confidence**.
- Exams and grades introduce an element of **competition** into the music.

Required?

If your child doesn't like jumping hurdles (and if you don't think that should be changed), don't send him to a school that requires taking exams to pass to a next level. Taking exams can work well for many, but they're not essential for a fruitful musical education, as millions of musicians can testify.

Scary

Are exams scary? Not if you love taking them. For others, they always will be, even though board examiners are expected to make accommodations in order to reduce fear, and to encourage candidates to play to the best of their abilities. To help young students get used to taking exams, there are special exams that they can't fail. Chapter 10 has tips to deal with or reduce exam nerves.

Fees

For information on exam fees, see page 115.

COMPETITIONS

Besides band competitions, there are all kinds of competitions for individual musicians. Some are intended to select musicians for an ensemble or a school, for example. Some offer a monetary prize for the winner exclusively. Some present all participants with no more than score sheets and constructive comments from the jury. And some award prizes for everyone — which turns the event in a positive experience for all.

Pros and cons

Most of the pros and cons of taking exams also go for participating in competitions. Children get to play for and be judged by persons other than their teacher, which may be very enlightening as long as the criticism is strictly constructive. At a competition, children will meet other students who are often just as nervous as they are (which may be a consolation or make things even worse), and what they hear other children play may inspire them to play even better — or frustrate them so much that they want to quit right away. What to do? Have a good look at your child and talk things over; try to figure out what seems best for him or her. Or have them give it a shot and see what happens before, during, and after the event. A tip: Some children participate in competitions to get used to playing in front of judges so that taking an exam becomes a less fearful event!

The teacher

Teachers should be able to properly judge their students' levels before enlisting them in a competition or exam; this prevents students from feeling needless frustration and failure.

Band competitions

For drum corps and various other types of bands, competing is a major part of the musical experience. There's more about these and other types of bands in Chapter 8.

4. PRACTICING

Many children (as well as adults and even professional musicians) don't like to practice. Why? Because people want to play their favorite music, rather than spending hours playing scales, etudes, or arpeggios. Because, oftentimes, progress doesn't show right away. Because learning to play an instrument is about long-term gratification, and we seem to have lost touch with that concept. Or because... A number of reasons. But still, it needs to be done — and it can be entertaining, too!

This chapter offers helpful hints on how to practice efficiently, which can be rewarding and inspiring. Ineffective practice habits are as much work as effective ones, but yield no progress and may cause children to quit playing. Also included is vital information on where and when to practice, the various components of a good practice session and how to structure it, practice techniques, memorizing music, and much more. Having some insight in these matters will make it easier for you to guide your children in this essential part of their music education.

Sports
Practicing is to music what training is to sports, but there are some major differences. Firstly, most sportsmen train with their teammates, while practicing is something you usually do alone. Secondly, if you play football, soccer, or any other type of sport, you'll probably have a match every week. Most musicians don't have that many opportunities to perform — and usually, being able to perform is why you practice in the first place.

Joining a band

That's why it's important for kids to join a band or an orchestra: It offers performance opportunities, it's a great way to meet new friends, and it provides your children with clear and realistic goals. Practicing so you can play your part at the next rehearsal is a better motivation than practicing because, well, you're supposed to.

One note

Joining an ensemble is even more important for children who play violin, cello, flute, saxophone, or any of the other instruments that typically produce one note at the time. These instruments are best suited for group settings, or should at least be accompanied by a piano, for example.

Chords

It's a bit different if you play the piano, guitar, keyboard, or other instrument on which you can produce both chords (several notes at once) and a melody at the same time. These instruments can be readily played without a band or other accompaniment. This situation tends to make practicing by yourself more musically rewarding.

Keep on going

It's clear that practice is necessary to achieve a certain level. But should children continue to practice once they've reached a level they're satisfied with? Maybe not, if they're at a point where they can perform at a level that satisfies them (and they'll get better simply by continuing to play). But oftentimes kids will find themselves restricted to playing the same pieces again and again. If boredom sets in, the end of their musical endeavors may be near.

No practicing

So can you play without practicing? Of course you can. There are many garage band musicians who never practice; they just play with their friends, and they're having a ball doing so. However, they will usually stop playing once they get a little older, and having no real musical basis, it's unlikely that they'll pick up an instrument again later on in life.

Recreational music making

Participating in a drum circle, for example, allows anyone

to play music with a group of people without any prior experience. These and other *recreational music-making* activities are about socializing, reducing stress, and relaxation more than striving for musical prowess. (Incidentally, that's what most garage bands are about, too.)

Not another obligation

For children who want to pursue a career in music, their practice habits should foster diligence, hard work, and making sacrifices (though the latter may not be considered as such). For all other children, practicing should be more fun than obligation, as pressure and taking things too seriously make the fun go away. But what if they don't want to practice? Shouldn't you exert at least a *little* pressure?

Means, goal, or making music?

Some tend to see practice as a goal in and of itself; and the goal is achieved by practicing, say, a half an hour a day. Others consider practice a means to an end — the end usually being the ability to play well (at whatever level) and to perform successfully. You can also consider practice as making music, as a journey that leads to who knows where, and the journey itself is what it's all about. For students who have teachers whose assignments (both in quantity as in quality) inspire them to play, and who get them to really understand why playing scales or practicing rudiments is essential (because that understanding usually makes this part of practice less of a drag) — there may be no need for pressure. The more a student considers practice to be a goal in itself, the more pressure you may need to apply to keep them practicing. That said, almost every child needs to be pushed a little from time to time.

HOW LONG — OR HOW?

One of the most frequently asked questions is, "How long should my child practice?" You could certainly structure it to last a required number of minutes per day. But wouldn't it be more interesting to look at what should or could be achieved, so a student's focus would be on accomplishing a particular task, rather than simply filling time? Still, no matter how you look at it, a child must invest some time in practice, and it's essential to be able to gauge how much time that typically is; so that's what the next section addresses.

Three to six

Most experts seem to agree that you can't really speak of 'practicing' when kids are three to six years of age. For this age group, it's more about spending quality time and having fun with the instrument (if they've actually already chosen one) than about trying to achieve something other than a long-lasting love for music. For most of these children, playing up to five or ten minutes a day will be fine. The shorter these sessions last and the more fun they are, the more likely your child will want to play three, four, or more days per week.

Six and up

As children get a little older, they'll be able to focus for longer periods, and they'll start to grasp the concept of doing things now that will pay off later. They will also be ready to maintain a practice routine with their teacher's and your guidance. Six- to eight-year-olds should typically spend some fifteen minutes per day on an instrument, for anywhere from four to six days per week. The older they get, the longer they will be able, and willing, to play. Children of twelve and up are usually expected to play about a half an hour a day or more. If they practice effectively, however, they may be able to do their assignments in less time (which can be so rewarding that they end up playing even longer!).

Short and often

A practice session lasting a half an hour can be quite long for most kids, so it's often better to divide the routine up into three ten-minute sessions, or even six sessions of five minutes each. Short sessions tend to be more effective, with improved retention and more focus.

Much longer

The better you get, the more you need to practice to progress and maintain your abilities at a desired level. Music majors often practice three to five hours a day. The longer you practice, the sooner you will find that not practicing decreases your abilities — so you have to keep up all, or most, of the time!

Music, not minutes

For students to focus on the music rather than the minutes passing by, they must understand exactly what their teacher expects, and be able to self-assess whether they've achieved the goals set for the next lesson. This requires that teachers be very explicit about assignments. For example, rather than simply telling a student to "learn to play that piece," they must state specific criteria, (i.e., "play it with the metronome at 148 beats per minute," or "play a scale five times, without any mistakes, at a certain minimum tempo"). This way, students know when they've completed the assignment. If the teacher also conveys the practice techniques they'll need to most effectively reach the goals set for that week, practicing can be much more than a thirty-minute routine to be endured. This also puts things into the students' own hands: If they practice efficiently, they'll finish quickly; and if they finish real quickly, they can even decide to take a day off. Or they might be inspired to do more than they were asked to in the first place.

Your own teacher

Practicing is something that needs to be learned (and taught). When you practice alone, you're expected to catch your own mistakes, to discover what prompted them, to fix them, and to find a way to prevent them in the future. In effect, when you practice, you are your own teacher. That's not an easy thing to be.

At home

And after all that, when you get to your next lesson, you sometimes realize that you're not able to play what you could play at home. Or could you? Did you really hear everything that went wrong? Did you repeat everything to a point where you could even play it under pressure? Probably not — and playing in front of your teacher, or anyone else, is quite different from playing when no one is around. That's why it's good for parents to ask their children to play for them every now and then, or at the end of each practice session, or perhaps as a weekly routine. Getting experienced in how to play for others is an important part of the learning process.

WHEN

Ideally, practicing becomes a daily routine; something which is as natural as having dinner, or brushing your teeth. And just like most people have dinner or brush their teeth around the same time every day, practicing is more likely to become a natural part of the day when you do it at or around a set time. Getting children used to spending some time with their instrument on a regular basis may be more important than how much practice they actually do, initially.

Every day?

Should children practice every day? It's unlikely that anything you *have* to do seven days a week will be a lot of fun. That's why most experts will advise you that five to six days a week will be sufficient to make progress. With one lesson and five days of practice, your child is still playing six days a week.

Which day?

The Sunday is the one that's most likely to be your child's preferred day off, but you may point out that this day allows for more time to practice than most other days in the week, and that practicing still leaves plenty of time for other activities. You can also leave it up to your children to pick their day off per week.

(Not) making it up

Should kids occasionally miss any of the other days, you may consider not asking them to make it up. Skipping a day now and then is no disaster. You may try to inspire children to practice a little more the day before their 'extra' day off, however. Tip: The day before the lesson is usually the worst one to skip.

A closer look

It's often very effective to have a short practice session right after the lesson or later that same day. This reinforces the lesson content, and it's a perfect opportunity for you

and your child to take a close look at the weekly assignments. Be around, if possible, and make sure your child
understands everything he or she has to do that week. If
anything is unclear, you or your child can get in touch
with the teacher and ask for additional information.

No time?

On days that are too busy to do the entire practice routine,
you may suggest children to just play one of their favorite
pieces, or something else they like play, as long as they
keep in touch with the instrument. A tip: Suggest them to
play for just two or maybe three minutes — and they may
end up playing longer.

When?

Many kids like the security of practicing at a set time or
moment of the day (before school, right after school,
before dinner…), especially when they're too young to know
how to schedule their time. Others prefer to schedule
their practice time around other obligations. That way,
they can play when they feel like it, rather than having to
do so because it happens to be 4:00 PM. Here are some
additional tips on planning practice sessions:

- Practicing **before doing homework** provides a nice break
  between your child's academic activities, but it may be
  hard to focus on music if there's a lot of homework to be
  done.
- Waiting until **after homework** to practice may feel as if
  you're never finished; it's like one obligation after the
  other.
- Some kids love to practice **before going to school**.
- Planning a practice session before their **favorite TV
  show** (which is then the reward for practicing) may be
  more successful than asking them to play after that
  show.
- If **weekday practice sessions** are prompted by your
  child's school day schedule — for example, practicing
  before or after school — then make sure he or she has
  practice cues for weekends and holidays as well (after
  church, before dinner, etc).
- If there's **more than one child** at home, have each one
  practice while the others do their homework (provided
  the practice noise doesn't disturb the latter). Playing

scales when you know your siblings are watching TV is usually harder than when you realize they're doing math.

Holidays

It's really important that children keep to their practice sessions during school holidays. If they don't touch their instrument for three or more weeks, the first lessons and practice sessions after the holiday will most likely be highly frustrating — they probably won't be able to play those same pieces anymore. You may consider negotiating a holiday schedule with them: for example, playing four instead of six days a week, or suggest that they practice first-thing after breakfast, leaving the rest of their day wide open. This is also a perfect time for practicing on weekend days!

How?

Children have their own ways of handling assignments, most likely approaching them the same way they do other things in life. Teachers should recognize these individual styles and help students use apply their styles to their practice sessions to make them as efficient as possible. Some examples:

- Children who're not good at **focusing** their attention should not be assigned three new pieces at once.
- Children who are **afraid** to start a new piece, may tend to 'practice' pieces they already play very well. They're dedicating time to practicing, but without progress.
- Children who aren't aware of **their own mistakes** will end up rehearsing those mistakes, and it'll be hard to reverse and 'deprogram' the errors. These students need to learn how to evaluate their own playing before moving on.
- Children who **skip sections** they can't play should be treated differently than those who keep repeating things without getting any further.

Discuss

If you feel your child's practice habits aren't as fruitful as they could be, or if you notice that any of the problems mentioned above are occurring frequently, you should discuss how to handle this with his or her music teacher.

Sitting in

Do you need to be around when your child is practicing? Young children often don't like being alone when they play. Just being there might be comforting to them (as long as you're not distracting them); so read a book, pay the bills... Children may also appreciate it if you're actively involved — so sit with them, listen to every note they play, read along with the music, and help them out when they get stuck. It is unrealistic to expect that children under the age of ten can plan, organize, and maintain an effective practice session all alone.

Progress

If you simply want to keep an eye on your child's progress, you might just join them for a couple of minutes of each practice session. Recurrent recitals, as discussed on page 83, are good ways to keep in the loop, but it might be better to actually watch your child practice, from time to time. You'll learn how they manage their time, tackle problems, and so on. This can also be a valuable source of information for their teacher. If your child doesn't like having you around during practice time, simply leave well alone. You can still hear how things are going. After all, most practice rooms aren't really soundproof.

Judge

If a teacher specifies that your child should be able to play something particular by the end of the week (or a couple of days after the lesson, etc.), it may be up to you to assess whether or not that goal has been achieved. As children mature they will hopefully develop the ability to self-evaluate their own playing. Tip: Suggest to your children that they record themselves playing the assigned piece; then have them judge their performance for themselves based on the recorded result. This is very instructive for musicians at any level. (There's more on this on page 176.)

WHERE

Ideally, children should be able to practice at any time of the day, without being hindered and without hindering others (see page 75). A space needn't be large, just enough to accommodate your child and the instrument. If there's room for the instrument to remain unpacked between practice sessions, no valuable time (or inspiration!) gets lost by having to unpack and assemble it before each practice. Your child should be able to grab the instrument, tune it if necessary, and play. There are various types of floor-standing and wall-mounted stands on which string, wind, and other small instruments can sit unpacked and out of the way of people and pets and other damaging circumstances. Special covers are also available to help protect your valuable investments against dust and air-borne dirt.

Music stand

For students who read sheet music, a stand is necessary. A music stands is a very affordable piece of hardware that promotes good posture (and prevents sore necks), provided it has been set up correctly for your child. Nearly all music stands can be folded into a compact size, but it's easier if they can be left standing for the next practice session. (This also enhances their life expectancy, as they're often quite flimsy.) Is your child required to bring a stand to lessons or recitals? Then invest in a second stand to be kept in the instrument case or bag, if possible (that way, your child can't forget to bring it). A basic music stand will set you back less than twenty dollars. Tip: Most music stands have two 'arms' that keep the sheet music in place and prevent music books from flopping closed. If yours doesn't, you can use a rubber band or clothes pins, or you can have your lesson books spiral-bound so that they stay open. One more tip: Music stands are also available in bright colors and heavy-duty versions.

Light

Lighting in the room should be sufficient to see the music easily and clearly. An additional small lamp is usually all that takes. Tip: There are special lamps available for music stands specifically.

Stool or chair

A regular stool or chair will do for students of most instruments. Pianists, keyboard players, drummers, and other musicians benefit from a special (preferably height-adjustable) stool or bench. Without it, posture will be bad and practicing will be tiresome.

Metronome

A metronome is a small mechanical or electronic device that ticks or beeps out a steady, adjustable pulse. It's an important practice aid that prevents musicians from speeding up or slowing down the tempo, helping to develop one's inner clock. It's also a great device to use when practicing entire pieces or difficult bits very slowly (see page 87). It can also help you to improve your speed on the instrument step by step. Like any other tool, metronomes should be used wisely. Using one isn't a very good idea with a new piece, or when you're focusing on your tone, for example. Also, if you use it too often, you may become dependent on it. Metronomes are available starting at less than twenty dollars. Many electronic versions also sound a 440 Hz tuning tone (the standard A to which most instruments are tuned).

Two mechanical and two electronic metronomes.

Electronic tuner   Tipcode KIDS-001

Guitar students usually rely on electronic tuners to help them tune to the correct pitches. The more advanced types of tuners have a display that indicates which note (string) is being played, and whether it is *flat* (too low; the string needs to be tightened a bit) or *sharp* (too high; the string should be loosened a bit). Tuners are also used by wind instrument players and other musicians to check intonation. A decent tuner will set you back some twenty dollars or more. Some models double as a metronome. Orchestral string players and other musicians often prefer using a *tuning fork*. This is a short, two-pronged fork that produces an A (or another specified pitch) when you tap it on your knee, and gently put the stem against your ear or on the bridge of your instrument.

Sound systems and computers

Having a sound system in the practice area allows your child to play along to prerecorded music, play back a recorded lesson, or maybe even record the practice session. Likewise, a computer can be used to play back CDs, DVDs, and CD-ROMS; to access Internet lessons and music games; or to record practice sessions (if equipped with the right hardware and software). It's also a helpful tool to compose, arrange, transpose, or create music. Synthesizers, home keyboards, and other digital instruments can be hooked up directly to the computer using MIDI, the *musical instrument digital interface* that is part of all digital music equipment.

AND MORE

There's much more you, your child, and teachers can do to make practice more effective and fun. Here are some additional tips:

- Make sure that you know when your child is **extremely busy at school**, and consider lightening up on practice arrangements that week. You may also ask the teacher to take periods of heavy school workloads into account.
- "Have you **played** the piano yet?' Sounds different from, "Have you practiced yet?"
- Some children love playing in **another room** of the house from time to time, or even outside, if possible.
- Make sure practice time is **uninterrupted**. Ask friends who call to call back, and ask siblings to stay out of the way.
- Varying a child's assignments can help to **keep things fresh**. Some teachers focus on playing a new piece for a month or so, then address sound production or intonation for a couple of weeks, and so on.
- Make sure the teacher knows and **understands your child**. Some children love being told what to do, while others prefer to have a say in things.
- If your child often forgets certain parts of the weekly assignments, or seems to misunderstand the teacher's

instructions, suggest to the teacher to have the child write down their assignment themselves, in **their own words**.

- If older kids wants to practice at least an hour a day, have them take one or more **short breaks** within that hour.
- Even shorter **micro-breaks** help kids of any age stay focused. If you just can't get that one difficult passage down, comb your hair, pet the cat, eat a carrot, take a sip of water… or whatever before trying again. Or try again next week!
- The instrument should be in good repair and **tuned properly**. If your child can't tune his or her instrument yet, learn to do it yourself. Ask the teacher for help or consult the relevant Tipbook (see pages 191–195).
- Practicing with **play-along recordings** is often a lot more fun than practicing band or orchestra parts by yourself. There are commercially available play-along media, but another option is to record a performance or rehearsal of the band or orchestra your child is in, and use that.
- **Stop if it hurts**. Playing an instrument should not induce pain. If the pain (back, fingers, neck, lips — anywhere) returns every time your child practices or plays, consult the teacher. The solution could be as simple as getting a different chair or resetting the music stand.

REDUCING THE SOUND LEVEL

Listening to a beginner practice is usually not very agreeable. Also, practicing seriously sometimes means playing loudly. And on some instruments, playing softly is something that takes time to learn.

Headphones

Instruments that need an amplifier to be heard can be absolutely silent during practice. Simply turn the volume way down, or turn the speaker off completely and plug in a pair of headphones.

Most electronic keyboard instruments (digital pianos, keyboards, etc.) have one or two headphone outputs. The second one is useful for lessons (one for the student, one for the teacher), or to be able to play four-handed pieces. Practice amps for electric guitars and basses usually have a headphone output too; alternatively, you can plug into a *guitar preamp* or *bass preamp* (a small box that usually features a number of guitar or bass effects) equipped with a headphone output. Tip: Keep the headphone volume level low to prevent hearing damage.

A small, affordable amplifier with a headphone output.

From recorder to drums

Acoustic instruments are those that do not need to be amplified, as they produce sound by themselves. The lowest sound levels are generated by recorders, violins, and acoustic guitars. The cello and the double bass (a.k.a. *upright bass* or *string bass*) sound about as loud, but they also generate contact noise as they rest on the floor (the sound travels throughout the house and possibly to your neighbors' through floors and walls). The flute, clarinet, oboe, French horn, tuba, and trombone sound a bit louder. The piano produces a sound level similar to these instruments, but in addition quite a bit of contact noise. Drums are by far the loudest of acoustic instruments, and with the bass drum pedal and hi-hat pedal, drum kits produce more contact noise than any other instrument.

Neighbors and housemates

So what can you do to keep neighbors and housemates happy if your child chooses to play one of the louder acoustic instruments? One effective solution is to limit practice times to hours when neighbors and housemates won't be bothered, if possible.

The source

The next best solution is to reduce the sound output, which you can do with most, but not all, instruments. The clarinet, the oboe, and the flute are three of the instruments that cannot be effectively muffled.

Brass instruments

For most brass instruments, there are various types of *mutes* that close off the bell of the instrument. Mutes are removable muffles or baffles that feature one or more tiny holes that allow very little sound to come though — generally quieting the instrument enough so as not to disturb anyone outside the room you're in. You have to adjust your playing when using a mute, though: You'll need to blow harder, as the mute will raise the pitch slightly — so it's not a good idea to use it routinely. A more expensive option is the Yamaha Silent Brass system: a plastic mute with a built-in microphone, a small amplifier, and a pair of headphones. The amp has an input for a cassette or CD player, so you can silently play along with prerecorded music. You can also hook up a second Silent Brass, or a home keyboard, for instance. A built-in reverb adds some space and life to the sound.

A trumpet practice mute.

Strings

There are two solutions for violinists and cellists: One is using a practice mute: a short, thick 'comb' that slides over the bridge of the instrument where it effectively mutes most of the sound — so it's best not to use one if you're working on your tone. The second solution, which is not usually considered very suitable for beginners, is a Silent Violin or a Silent Cello. These instruments don't have a sound-reinforcing body, but instead feature a small built-in amplifier and a headphone output. An audio input allows your child to hook up an audio player to play along to prerecorded music.

Designed for silent practice: the Silent Violin (Yamaha).

Saxophones

Most saxophone mutes (a padded ring, or an ordinary towel, that you insert into the bell) aren't very effective. They make the lowest notes difficult to play, while higher notes will hardly be dampened at all. After all, most of the tone holes are wide open when you play high notes, so muffling the far end of the instrument has no real use. A more effective alternative is a special bag that completely covers the instrument, considerably cutting down the volume. You play the horn using the three openings of the bag: one for each hand, and one for your mouthpiece. There are electronic wind instruments with a saxophone-style keywork and mouthpiece, but they're quite different from a genuine saxophone.

Piano

Many upright pianos have a *muffler pedal* or *practice pedal*. This pedal is located between the other two pedals. Pressing it makes a strip of felt move between the piano's strings and its hammers, muffling the sound to a certain extent. Many pianos now come with a built-in digital piano. These instruments are known as *hybrid pianos*. The digital sound, heard through speakers or headphones, can be triggered using the regular keys, after lowering a special bar that prevents the hammers from hitting the strings. Alternatively, you could get a digital piano next to or instead of an acoustic piano. Though they are still quite different instruments, the gap between them is lessening.

Drums

There are various solutions for drummers. First, most drum exercises can be done with an almost soundless practice pad; you can build an entire drum set with such pads, including the cymbals. Second, acoustic drums can be stuffed with blankets and cushions, or the plastic drum heads can be replaced with soundless mesh heads. The latter solution is more expensive, but yields less sound and a better 'feel.' If the same drum set is used in rehearsals or performances as well, it's better to muffle heads and cymbals with special rubber discs that can easily be removed. The most expensive, yet musically most satisfying, solution is to buy a set of electronic drums. Even then, the pedals may still cause contact noise problems.

An electronic drum set (Roland).

Someplace else

It's always best to practice an acoustic instrument without mufflers, mutes, or other sound-reducing accessories. So if sound is a problem, consider finding a formal practice space somewhere outside of the house (which is not an option for young kids, of course). For example, schools and music schools may have practice cubicles that you can use.

Soundproof rooms

Alternatively, it may be possible to soundproof a room or have a prefab soundproof studio installed. Both solutions are quite costly.

HEARING PROTECTION

Most children's daily practice sessions aren't long enough to cause hearing problems. The drums, again, are an exception to this rule: Playing them for fifteen minutes or even less a day could induce irreparable hearing damage, unless the drummer wears some kind of hearing protection.

Bands and orchestras

Hearing protection may also be necessary if your kids play in a band or an orchestra. A rehearsing rock band definitely sounds loud enough to more than justify such aids. You may have a hard time convincing your kid to wear some kind of protection, however. Presenting hearing protection as a cool thing will take a lot of effort (it would probably take endorsements from well-known artists who suffer from hearing loss; there are plenty of them around, unfortunately). Horn sections in bands and orchestras also produce enough sound to cause hearing damage, not only for players but for those sitting or walking directly in front of them as well. Tip: MP3 players and similar devices, when used at high volumes with headphones, also cause a lot of hearing damage among youngsters.

Solutions

Foam earplugs, available at drugstores and hardware stores,

Some affordable types of ear plugs.

are the cheapest form of hearing protection, but they cause a very muffled, unclear, and unnatural sound to be heard. Custom-made plugs with replaceable or adjustable filters protect without reducing sound quality, but are the most expensive solution. In between are various types of plugs, with or without special filters, available from most music stores. They usually come in a variety of standard sizes.

THE COMPONENTS

One of the main keys to effective practice is to have well-structured practice sessions. Depending on the student's level of playing, the main components of a practice session are:

- Warming up
- Scales and arpeggios
- Etudes
- Sight-reading
- New pieces
- Review

For beginning students, the list is shorter, with elements being added as they progress.

Tuning

Most instruments need to be tuned, or the tuning needs to be checked, before you can play. This is where the practice session really begins. As said before, it is easiest if the instrument is always ready to be played — unpacked and assembled. You may want to have valuable and vulnerable instruments packed when they're not being played, however. Also, parts such as strings, and the leather pads on woodwind instruments, tend to last longer if the instrument is covered in between practice sessions.

Warming up

Playing music requires a warm up, just like sports do: Advanced and professional musicians can even get injured from playing demanding pieces without a decent warm up. For beginners and intermediate players, the few minutes of 'warming up' are basically meant to get into mood for playing, to get the fingers going, and to get 'into the instrument.' It even helps if you take a good long look at your instrument before you play your first notes.

Warm-up exercises are not technically demanding; they're the ideal setting for focusing on tone quality, because you can really listen to the sound you're producing.

Scales, arpeggios and etudes

Tipcode KIDS-002

Scales and *arpeggios* (broken chords) are often used for warm ups, but they're also practiced separately. They're technical exercises that increase your playing proficiency, so your fingers will be able to do what your mind tells them to. *Etudes* are pieces written with that same goal in mind.

More fun

Many kids vehemently dislike scales, etudes, and similar exercise material; they're not as much fun as 'real' pieces, and they often seem meaningless. A good teacher might be able to make your child understand why they're so essential, inspiring them to play them with all their heart (though a little less will usually do). Besides, there are various ways to make playing them more fun. Some ideas?

- Focusing on your tone really helps; imagine what a scale would sound like when played by your **all-time favorite musician**!
- Playing scales as if they were **beautiful pieces of music** makes a difference too.
- Make the **volume go up** as you play the scale upwards, and vice versa.
- **Speed up** when playing upwards, and vice versa.
- Speed up *and* **get louder** one way, and vice versa.
- Play scales in **the rhythm of a song** you like, or play them as triplets.
- Pianists: Play F-major with **your left hand** and C-major with **your right hand**, and experiment with other pairs of scales.

New pieces

Adding new pieces is necessary to keep students progressing, to keep them challenged, to expand their repertoire, and to raise their general level of playing. Check pages 87–89 for tips on handling new pieces.

Reviewing repertoire

When you play pieces you already know, there's no

struggle, so you're simply playing music. It's as close to performing as practicing will get — and that's what playing is all about, for most students. Reviewing older pieces also keeps their repertoire alive.

Sight-reading
Sight-reading is as essential part of various exams and competitions: You're given a new and unfamiliar piece of music to read and play on demand. It's much the same as reading a story or an article to someone, albeit that playing while reading music is quite a bit harder than reading text aloud. Sight-reading is an important skill for all musicians who want or need to play in situations where you'll be expected to perform or rehearse without prior preparation.

And more
A practicing session can consist of lots of other components, such as:
- **Specific exercises** (dynamics, phrasing, bowing, improvisation, ear training, extending your range with higher or lower notes, etc.).
- Experimenting: **Explore the instrument**, try to discover new sounds or playing techniques, try to figure out a melody you've heard, think up new melodies…
- **Play along** with prerecorded music. Numerous self-taught players learned their instrument this way, and it's a valid, fun, and effective technique for any musician who doesn't have a band or an orchestra at their disposal.

Recitals
A short recital, in which your kid plays (a section of) a new piece or an older song for you, can make a great practice session finale. Children will get the opportunity to perform, and you'll hear how they've progressed. Also, playing 'in public' on a regular basis can help diminish performance anxiety and teach them to continue playing through mistakes. Generally, when the teacher is the first to hear a new song, most children make mistakes they didn't make when they played it at home; so short recitals help prepare them for playing for their teacher. A recital once a week will usually do, but some children will want you to listen to them every day.

Family and friends

Note that children who love to perform for you may not want to do so for family or friends; and the ones who do now may say no as they near their teen years and become more self-conscious. Forcing them to play is probably the best way to make them quit entirely (or perhaps trade in their violin for a drum set).

Maintenance

Depending on the instrument, a couple of minutes at the end of each practice session should be dedicated to daily instrument maintenance.

Wind instruments have to be disassembled and dried, orchestral string instruments will need the hair of their bows slackened, guitar and bass guitar strings need to be cleaned, and so on. Specific instructions can be found in the Tipbooks on the most popular instruments (see pages 191–195).

STRUCTURE

Your child's assignments will indicate what needs to be done for the week, and a good teacher will also tell them (or you) the best approach to take. Your role, depending on your child's age and degree of independence, will be to help structure their practice sessions: Most children are unable to effectively plan fifteen minutes or half an hour of activities.

Time management

Make sure your young children's practice sessions are given a permanent slot in their daily routine along with school, homework, seeing friends, sports, watching TV, chatting, and other activities. Time management is something they need to be taught.

The beginning

It's usually best to start with things that are relatively easy to play, such as scales. Some prefer to start their sessions with a piece they already know. Doing the hard stuff first may be an effective way to handle homework, but when it comes to music, starting off with an unfamiliar piece can be quite frustrating.

The end and in between

Ending the session with a review of their older repertoire is like a reward for having practiced: They get to play something they know and that they've worked on before. In between, the choice is basically up to the student or you, and their teacher might have helpful suggestions based on the child's learning style or way of practicing. A tip: Some students prefer the safety of doing things in the same order every time, while others dislike such routine and would rather vary the order of their practice components from day to day.

Two or three sessions

If practice time is divided into two or more sessions, it'll probably be most effective to do a little of everything in each session rather then spending the first session only on scales, the second on a new piece, the third on older repertoire, etc. — but then your child might just prefer that.

Clock?

Some experts advise you to dedicate a certain amount of time to each component: a five minute warm-up, ten minutes or etudes, ten on the new piece, and another five to play something familiar. Others will tell you to get rid of the clock, as you want children to focus on what they're playing rather than on the minutes passing by. But without a clock present, you should probably see to it that your child doesn't spend half an hour playing scales (right!), so there's no time left for the other assignments. If the assignments have been structured well and the teacher has provided your child with checkpoints, this will probably not happen. Still, it's good to keep an eye on things; you might want to listen in and jot down how much time your child spends on warming up, on scales, and so on.

Goals

For older children, it can be helpful to talk about the goals they've set for each practice session apart from those set by their teacher. When they're old enough, they can start setting their own goals.

Short, medium, long

The clearer one's goals are, the easier it will be to practice effectively. When defining goals, it often helps to distinguish:

- **long-term goals** (I'd like to join such-and-such band, or play a solo recital by the end of the year, or become a professional musician);
- **mid-term goals** (I'd like to finish this book, or be able to play these pieces);
- and **short-term goals**, which may differ for each practice session (I'd like to memorize this piece, or play that section ten times without a mistake).

PRACTICING TECHNIQUES
Practicing efficiently is also a matter of applying the right practicing techniques. Improving your tone requires a different technique than increasing your speed, or tackling a new piece.

Small jobs
One of the best ways to make your practice session more effective and fun is to break down large jobs into a number of small jobs. Rather than tackling a new piece from beginning to end, break it down into four or eight measures to be played per day, for example. This way, the student can have a small success every day, rather than fighting to master the entire piece in one week.

Revision
If a new piece is broken up into sections comprised of a number of bars, reviewing the sections that were done on previous days should be an essential part of each practice session. Learning an instrument is most effectively done through frequent repetition. (In various languages, the word for 'practice' literally means repetition!)

The right notes
Repetition results in long-term memory storage, which is good. The problem, however, is that your memory does not select what should be stored and what should not: If you consistently repeat an incorrect passage, that's what will be stored. If you play the wrong note half of the time, there's a fifty-fifty chance that the wrong note will come out at your performance. So when repeating things, make sure you play the right notes.

Five or ten

Some teachers may advise you to move to the next section only when you're able to play the current section correctly five (or ten) times in a row. If you make a mistake, you start counting all over again — until you get all five (or ten) correct. Others may not be concerned with the number of repetitions, so long as you play it right the final time — so that your fingers 'remember' the right moves.

Slow down

A difficult passage may be hard to play correctly, and playing it right five times in a row may seem impossible. The solution is to slow things down. Slow, in this case, means really slow. Take one, two, or more seconds for every note, and disregard note values for now. Take a metronome, set it at sixty BPM (i.e., sixty Beats Per Minute, equaling one beat per second), and let it tick one, two, or more times before moving on to the next note. Such slow tempos make you aware of the movements your fingers have to make to get from note to note, or from chord to chord.

Tone

For advanced players, practicing a piece really slowly is also a good way to work on their tone, and to get the smallest nuances of a piece right: dynamics, intonation, phrasing, and everything else beyond hitting the right notes at the right time.

A NEW PIECE

There are also various practicing techniques for handling new pieces. As mentioned before, a piece can be divided up into four bar, eight bar, or longer sections, revising the previous sections (and playing them absolutely correctly) before moving on. This is just one of many approaches, and all of these approaches can be mixed to come up with a combination that works well for your child.

Challenge

Starting a new piece is a positive challenge for some children, while it makes others feel as if they have to start all over again. A good teacher takes that into account, and any student will eventually understand that avoiding new pieces will yield no progress. Also, learning to tackle new pieces helps students to tackle other problems and to deal with new, complex subjects as well — which is one of the reasons that music students perform better in various academic fields. Some of the tips below apply to more advanced students only; others work for beginners too.

Listen

As said before, it is essential that you practice a piece playing only the correct notes. It helps if students can first listen to the music so they know what it's supposed to sound like before attempting to play it. The teacher can play a new piece for them, or they can listen to a recorded version.

Read along

Reading along while listening to a new piece helps students correlate the notes to the music. With complex pieces, study the part visually before listening to it, so you won't be surprised by repeats and other markings. Reading the music before playing it also gives you the opportunity to check out all dynamic signs and tempo markings, to locate accidentals (flats, sharps, naturals), and numerous other details and characteristics of the piece — and you don't have to worry about playing the instrument at the same time you're reading.

More

It's also helpful if the teacher tells the students about the music: the general character of the piece, its form (12-bar blues or 32-bar AABA? Rondo or suite?), the style, the composer, the era in which it was written, and so on. After all, there's more to music than playing the notes the composer wrote down.

Step by step

Beginning players are often advised to approach a new piece step by step. First, clap the rhythm of the notes, counting aloud as you go. When you've got the rhythm down, play the melody without paying attention to the rhythm. Once you can clap the rhythm and play the right notes, combine the two — very, very slowly. This approach works well for advanced players too. Pianists and other keyboard players can practice the left hand part first, and then the right hand, before attempting to play a new piece with both hands.

The trouble spots

Alternatively, depending on your ability and the complexity of the piece, you can play the piece through at an easy tempo, spotting the difficult bits as you go. Playing a piece as such, with mistakes and all, may give you a general idea of what it is about (assuming you haven't heard it before). Other players would rather start by locating the tricky bits then figuring them out first. A tip: If you're working on a tricky section, always include a few notes or bars before and after that particular section in order to make the tricky section a part of the whole thing, rather than an isolated hurdle that might scare you off as you get close to it.

Analyzing the trouble spots

If you're having a problem with a section, you can simply play it again and again (and again) until you get it right; but it might be more effective to find out what's causing the problem in the first place. Is it the fingering (which fingers to use for which note)? The rhythm? Or can you not play the part with your left hand while your right hand is doing something else? Or is it a note higher or lower than you can play or sing? Children may welcome your help in analyzing what the problem is: You are the one who's around when they get stuck; not their teacher. You don't need to play an instrument to help your kid identify the problem. All it takes is asking the right questions so they can figure it out on their own. One step beyond analyzing the trouble spots is developing exercises that help the student tackle them. This is something advanced players do for themselves, and something that teachers should teach their students.

MEMORIZING

Opinions differ as to whether students should memorize music or not. Some teachers insist that they should; others feel that memorizing music should be optional, unless a student is considering a professional career in music.

Why?

Why would a teacher require that your child learns to memorize a piece that can be simply read off of sheet music?

- It makes children **better musicians**. If you're not concentrating on which notes to play, you can fully focus on other elements — tone, phrasing, dynamics, and so on — and listen to yourself play. Also, to play from memory you have to *really* know a piece inside out, which can only help improve your performance.
- Guitarists, pianists (and other keyboard players), and harpists who play by heart can **watch their hands** as they play, which may be very helpful if they have to make big leaps. Not a very professional approach, but it can be handy.
- It makes you **look good**. Professional soloists play without sheet music, so why can't you?

Why not?

Of course, there's no need to keep students from memorizing music (and some are extremely good at it), but why force them?

- Being required to play without sheet music makes a performance an **even more stressful** event — and wasn't making music about enjoying yourself?
- **Worrying** about what'll happen if you forget the piece does not inspire a good performance. It takes away more energy from the music than reading notes does. In other words, some just need sheet music to play well, even while others might play better without it.
- For students who are not good at memorizing, learning pieces by heart will take up **valuable time** that's probably better spent on things they *can* do to improve and to grow musically. Forcing students to do things they don't like or are not good at can even make them want to quit (and of course, teachers and parents should be aware that in some cases, this is just typical reluctance that needs to be overcome).

Marching

Members of marching bands' drum lines are often required to memorize music, and the same usually goes for musicians in other bands where a 'choreography' or

The flip folder attaches to the wind instrument's lyre.

drill is an essential part of the performance: It is hard to play, move, and read at the same time. Some directors encourage their band members to play by heart, but don't force them to. A so-called 'flip folder,' which holds the sheet music, can be attached to any marching instrument.

Techniques and tips

There are various ways and techniques to memorize music. The best way depends on the student, the level of playing, and other factors. The shortlist below will help you recognize how your child handles things, and offers some suggestions.

- You can memorize a piece **as you learn it**, or you can wait to memorize it once you can play it correctly.
- Memorize **small sections** at a time. For some, a small section is one or two bars; for others, it's half a page. Start with the first section, and add subsequent sections only after you've mastered previous sections.
- Some memorize **the difficult parts** first, repeating them so often that they become as easy to play as the rest of the piece. Only after mastering the difficult parts do they include the other sections. Tip: Many teachers claim that you should never play a piece in any other order than the one intended.
- Most musicians memorize a piece from beginning to the end, but there are those who prefer to do it **the other way around**, working their way back to the beginning.
- You can also memorize bits and pieces **as you go**. Try not to look at the music while you're playing, glancing up only as you feel you need to. Bit by bit, over time, you will learn to play the entire piece by heart.
- If you repeat a piece or a section over and over, you're using your **finger memory** or tactile memory. Your fingers know what to do because they've been trained to

execute the patterns that are required for that piece of music. It's a relatively easy way to memorize, but it's not very reliable. Changing the tempo of the piece may confuse you (or your fingers). If you want to know if you've really memorized the music, play it at an extremely slow tempo and see what happens.

- Alternatively, you can **analyze the piece** step by step, studying every single aspect of it. This requires a lot of knowledge (scales, harmony, etc.), but it's the most reliable way to memorize.

- Practicing a piece **away from your instrument** may help you memorize it. Just play it in your imagination, first with, then without the music. This is referred to as *shadow practicing* or *armchair memorizing*. You can also try to hear the piece in your head without playing it, before you go to sleep, or on your way to school. Or sing it while you're taking a shower.

- It also helps if you **make up a story** that fits the music!

- **Slow practicing** is good for memorizing music.

- And when you're almost done, **put the book away**. Don't leave it on the music stand, pretending or trying not to peek, but put it in the other room. Out of sight, out of mind? Then try again.

5. GUIDANCE & MOTIVATION

Your guidance and support is essential to your child's music education. Because you see your child regularly, you will probably be able to spot any growing lack of interest in music much sooner than a teacher will. What can you do to guide your child and reduce the chance of him or her quitting?

First of all, it is important that you take your child's musical endeavors seriously. Show your interest by talking with them about their lessons, their teacher, their assignments, the pieces they play, the band director, their fellow band members, and so on. Try asking them questions that invite them to contemplate. Open questions like "What do you like best about your teacher?" or "What was it that you didn't like about that piece you had to play?" are more effective than questions that can be answered with a simple yes or no. Make this a recurring topic at the dinner table, while taking them to school, or any other opportunity for dialog. Also ask them about their assignments for the coming week, or ask them to play for you after their weekly lesson, so you know what they're up to... and so they know you that know.

Yell?

Children are usually not yelled at because they didn't watch TV, play with friends, or have fun. So should they be yelled at for not having practiced? That would make practicing too much like the other things most children would rather not do, from washing dishes to cleaning up the mess they made. It may be wiser to commend them for the little practice they *did* do. And when you hear them play, tell them what you liked or what you thought was really good, rather than hassling them about the mistakes they made.

Imposing a discipline

That doesn't mean you can't instill a sense of discipline. Many musicians, professional and amateur, are actually grateful that their parents made them practice. (And they still remember the trouble that caused, but "You chose to play this instrument, so…") Whether you want to go this route may depend on whether you see your child's musical activities as merely a hobby, or as an essential part of their education.

Positive feedback

Whichever way you handle this, positive feedback is always crucial if you want your child to keep on playing and enjoy doing so. Discussing your children's progress with their teacher in their presence can make them really proud.

Also try to keep track of their progress, and give them feedback: "This piece sounds a lot better now" or "Wasn't that the song you could not play two weeks ago? Great!" This is more effective than saying, "You did well today." The more specific you are, the more welcome and appreciated the compliment will often be.

Back off

Being asked, "Have you practiced?" every day can make your child want to stop completely. Backing off may help: Children may start practicing as soon as you stop nagging them. If you've noticed their enthusiasm at lessons and/or practice sessions has faded, perhaps backing off from attending these activities will help.

Co-teach?

Certain music programs require that parents be very actively involved in their children's education — parents are expected to be their children's home teacher. If your child is taking private lessons, however, you will usually not be expected to co-teach. In these situations, your genuine interest is most welcome, but you are encouraged not to interfere with your children's assignments or advise them to do things differently than what their teacher has told them to do. Your child will probably be confused if you do.

Different books
Likewise, if you plan to buy songbooks or method books other than those specified by the music teacher, call the teacher for suggestions or get their approval of a desired book before you buy. You are free to purchase whatever you want, of course, but getting the wrong books can contradict the teacher's methodology — and your child will end up suffering as a result. If children show a strong dislike toward the pieces their teacher is having them play, then listen to their arguments and talk to the teacher, rather than just substituting the teacher's selections with something the child wants, but the teacher hasn't approved.

Get to know the instrument
Another way to become involved is to take a few lessons on the instrument yourself. This will help you understand what your child is going through. You may even like it so much that you'll end up playing duets together... Also, children often appreciate your 'technical' assistance in the maintenance of their instrument, from changing strings to replacing and tuning drum heads.

Great motivator
Does your child have anyone to play with? Being in a band or an orchestra is one of the greatest motivators, and the opportunity to play duets with a neighbor or friend can have the same inspiring effect. You may even consider learning to play an instrument yourself, if you don't play already. There's more on the benefits of playing in an ensemble in Chapter 8, which also covers the various types of bands, orchestras, and other groups.

Rewards
Positive feedback is a great motivator, and so is success. Children also love rewards. As a parent, you know what inspires your child. Being allowed to pick what's for dinner, a visit to the cinema, or any other activity they like

can be the perfect rewards for their musical efforts. There are lots of music-related gifts, too: new strings for their guitar (having them replaced before they break is not a real luxury, but it sure can feel that way), a new drum head (same here), a nice reed holder, other accessories, a CD of their favorite artist, a concert ticket, and so on. You can turn one 'large' reward into a number of small, very affordable ones. Simply give them one or more colorful stickers for every single goal they achieve (mastering a scale or a new piece, finishing a book…) and promise them a CD of their choice when they have collected ten stickers, for example.

Awards
Children love tangible proof of their achievements, so many teachers have different ways of rewarding their students, such as a sticker or an ink stamp for every completed assignment. Others use different types of awards (e.g., one for every book a student completes) and certificates (e.g., for every year or two years of study). Tip: Offer to frame these precious papers for your child! Another tip: Make photos of your child practicing, or especially when they perform, either at home, or at a competition or a studio recital. These photos, plus things like the program from an event, can be collected and saved in a musical scrapbook for your child.

Contract
Another approach to keeping your child motivated to play: Have them sign a contract of their musical aspirations, promising in writing that they will stick with the chosen instrument for one or even two years, and that they'll complete their musical assignments every week. While many educators and parents strongly believe this works, you may wonder if you yourself would be willing to sign such a contract when you begin a new hobby. And do children have to sign contracts for other things they really *like* doing? Still, it may be a viable approach for kids who quit any new activity within a couple of weeks, or for children who feel that a contract proves that their plans are being taken really seriously. It goes without saying that really young children will not be able to grasp the concept of a contract.

Their own money

You could also consider having your child invest their own money into their instrument. Even if it's a dollar a month, this investment can make them aware of the value of the instrument, and it may keep them from quitting too easily.

Off days

Everyone has off days, and so do children. Forcing a child to play when he or she is really not in the mood may not be a good idea. The likelihood that any progress would be made in such cases is close to nil, and if music becomes an obligation, the fun may soon be gone. Still, it can't hurt to suggest that they play just one of their favorite songs that day — but if that doesn't work, let go.

More off days

If your child doesn't feel like playing more than once a week, or for a longer period of time, it's time to find out what's going on. Children will often say that they "just don't feel like it." Telling them to "feel like it" or be motivated won't really help either; you need to find out why they feel the way they do. The sooner you get to the bottom of their apathy, the more likely it is that you can turn things around and get them playing again. Some random thoughts:

- It might be that they don't like **the music they play** anymore. Musical preferences change over time.
- The same can go for **their teacher**. Someone could be your son's favorite teacher one day, then not the next. He may need someone new to inspire him.
- Some children want to quit because they're being **harassed** by fellow band members, or because the band director makes them feel insecure about their musical capabilities. These kinds of situations are difficult for children to reveal, so something of this nature could be behind their "just not feeling like it anymore."
- Also, the level of **musicianship** of the ensemble they're in may be too high (making them fear they'll fail) or too low (making them bored and uninspired).
- Your child may have serious **problems in reading music**, keeping him or her from progressing as fast as they otherwise could. A stronger focus on playing by ear and improvising may help.

- Musicians of all levels experience recurrent periods in which they **don't seem to progress**, as described on page 19. Telling your child that even professionals — and their favorite artists — go through such times may help. It is like hitting a plateau on your way up the mountain; you just walk while nothing happens. And then, all of a sudden, you find your way to the next plateau, with numerous new things to discover.

- **Shifting focus** is a technique that may help in periods of slow or no progress. If mastering new pieces seems to be the problem, it can be good to focus on tone production or technique for a while, or vice versa. A change of activities can help to keep things fresh and rewarding. Talk to your child's teacher!

- **Time management** may be a problem. If your child feels that practice sessions have to be squeezed in with loads of other activities, practicing will hardly ever be fun — it's just another thing that needs to be done. Help your child by scheduling things differently.

- If schoolwork demands most of their time because of **special projects or exams,** or in times of emotional stress, children may be grateful if you just let them play and enjoy their music, rather than expecting noticeable progress. Make sure their teacher knows, and do help them get back to their regular practice routine when things are back to normal.

- Make sure your child feels **free to speak up** when their music assignments are more then they can handle (or less than what's needed to keep them motivated!).

- There's no use practicing what you're good at, but the joy of making music will soon fade if children focus solely on what they're **not so good** at. If playing faster tempos is a problem, focusing too much on speed may be extremely frustrating. So why not have them play things they like? If that makes them play more, their agility will increase automatically.

- Do they still like **the instrument** they're playing? Chances are they might not if they were assigned an instrument rather than being allowed to choose their favorite. Regardless, a growing dislike of their current instrument will want to make them quit. As they may not be able to articulate this, you may hear, "I don't feel like it anymore" instead.

- Is their instrument in **good repair**? Does it make playing fun and easy? Does it allow them to grow musically? (See page 100.)
- Does your child have any **musician friends**? If all of their friends are playing ball, it may be hard to focus on scales and etudes.
- And if children really want to quit, you should perhaps **just let them**. You can be satisfied to have instilled a love of music in your child, but you can't force someone to love playing. Maybe, they'll pick up an instrument again later in life.

Danger zones

Kids could decide they want to stop playing anytime, but there are specific 'danger zones' to watch out for. The first is in or around the second half of the first year of lessons, as progress often slows and the excitement has worn. The second is around a child's twelfth year, when a lot of changes are taking place, as discussed on pages 13–14. Simply paying a little extra attention to your children may be enough to keep them playing!

6. BORROWING, RENTING, OR BUYING?

Your child wants to play an instrument, so you need to get one. Is it wise to borrow one from a friend? Does your child's school provide instruments, or should you rent, lease, or buy one? And if you do decide to rent or buy, where do you go? This chapter sheds some light on these topics, and provides information on the costs of playing an instrument — from maintenance and sheet music to band and exam fees.

If you want your child to enjoy playing, and have a fair chance to do so for many years, a good instrument is vital. Numerous children have quit because they had to practice on an out-of-tune piano with keys that stuck, or a leaky flute; for wind instruments, choosing the right mouthpiece for your child is essential; reed players need good reeds; and so on... Children cannot understand the limitations of a faulty instrument and will likely to blame themselves for any failure to play well. And once, however wrongfully, they're convinced they cannot play, they probably won't.

School and family instruments
Unfortunately, the instruments that you may borrow or rent from your child's school are not always in a decent state of repair. When in doubt, have the instrument assessed by the technician at your local music store, a musician who specializes in that instrument, or your teacher.

Value for money
The quality of new musical instruments has generally gone

up while prices have gone down; so today, you actually tend to get a lot of value for your money. A decent electric or acoustic guitar can be purchased for less than one hundred and fifty dollars, for example. Some instruments made for that little money are not of good quality, however. Flutes, clarinets, saxophones, and other wind instruments in that price range may be playable at first, if you're lucky, but it is usually impossible to adjust or repair them: keys go out of adjustment easily, bending or soldering could be damaging, and spare parts are unavailable. Such products are commonly referred to as 'ISOs,' or Instrument Shaped Objects.

Not all experts dislike these low-quality instruments. Some consider them workable enough options for children (who are known to change their minds on what they want to eat halfway through lunch, much less on which instrument they want to play) just trying out an instrument. Besides, the fact that it's their own, rather than rented, may be an extra motivator

Teachers
Many teachers will simply refuse to teach a child who brings an unplayable instrument to lessons. Of course, teachers will typically offer advice on renting or buying a proper instrument, as well as maintenance, beforehand. But be aware that teachers are sometimes not permitted to suggest where to buy or rent an instrument!

The best you can get
All instruments come in a wide range of prices. More expensive instruments usually offer a better sound, have a longer life expectancy, feature materials and craftsmanship of a higher quality, have a higher resale value, and, very importantly, they're usually easier to play than inexpensive models.

Still, while it's usually wise to buy the best instrument you can afford, it's probably not a good idea to buy your eight-year-old a six-thousand dollar saxophone.

Pro?
Many companies distinguish three quality categories for most musical instruments: beginner or student-line models, intermediate or step-up instruments, and professional

instruments. The first problem with such categorization is that they tell you virtually nothing about the actual cost of the instruments (for example, a 'student-line' bassoon costs a lot more than an 'intermediate' guitar). The second problem is that opinions differ as to the price ranges per category: What some call a step-up flute, is a beginner's instrument to others.

The third problem is that 'professional' is the number-one most misused word in the music industry. Many instruments with a 'pro' label are really made and priced for beginners. True professional instrument don't need such labels. Please refer to the various instrument Tipbooks for more information (see page 191–195).

How much?

If you plan to buy your child an instrument, most teachers will advise you not to purchase the least expensive one you can find, but to instead go for a decent, dependable instrument that your budding musician will enjoy for at least a couple of years. What do such 'decent' instruments cost, and how much is a cheap one? A tip in advance: Many schools own the more expensive types of instruments and provide them to their students, as you will read on page 104.

- A decent recorder would be one of the least expensive choices of instruments at around fifty dollars. You can get a plastic one for less than ten.
- Think two hundred dollars for an acoustic guitar, and even less for an electric one. The latter isn't complete, however, without another hundred to two for a practice amp, strap, and picks.
- Decent home keyboards start at around three hundred dollars. A good digital piano with a hammer action keyboard (see page 167) can cost three times as much.
- New acoustic pianos start around fifteen hundred dollars, but you're often better off with one of at least twice that price.
- Most woodwind instruments will set you back some five hundred dollars (but some stores sell flutes for less than two hundred, as mentioned before). Alto and tenor saxophones and oboes are more expensive, at around seven or eight hundred dollars. A bassoon easily costs three thousand dollars.

- Trumpets and other smaller brasswinds start at around two hundred dollars; expect to pay around five hundred or more for a step-up instrument. French horns are more expensive — student models often cost around seven or eight hundred dollars. A tuba can easily set you back about two thousand dollars.

- Few people buy their child a violin until they're ready for a full-sized instrument, at around the age of twelve or later. Decent, complete outfits (violin, bow, case) are typically around seven or eight hundred dollars (but you can find them as low as a hundred). Cello outfits cost more, and so do double basses.

- Step-up and professional drum sets are usually sold without cymbals. Expect to pay between one thousand and fifteen hundred dollars for a complete set (five drums, one or two cymbals, and a hi-hat), which is good enough for performance purposes; but you can find sets for less than three hundred as well.

Less and more

As the quality of low-priced instruments continues to increase, you may be able to buy a decent beginner's instrument for very little money. However, follow experts' advice to prevent disappointments: To the layman's eye, a forty dollar guitar may look exactly like a six-hundred dollar one, but the cheaper one may need to be retuned every five minutes, for example.

If you really have money to spend, the sky is the limit. You can easily spend a thousand dollars on a single cymbal; a handmade flute may cost fifty thousand or more (but it's hard to find a saxophone or a clarinet that costs more than ten!); a professional harp can cost thirty thousand; a grand piano may set you back two hundred thousand — and millions have been paid for Stradivarius violins or Guarnerius cellos.

BORROWING

The opportunity to borrow an instrument may be very tempting, but these instruments are often not the best ones. This goes especially for so-called 'family' instruments. Many types of wind instruments will be unplayable if they haven't been used and maintained for a couple of years or more, and the same goes for pianos. A technician will be able to tell you how much it will cost to get the instrument back into playing condition again. With the guitar, your chances are better that time will not have degraded its quality; and there are millions of guitars in attics eagerly waiting to be played again. Small children need a smaller-sized guitar, though, as discussed on page 131! If you borrow an instrument, you may want to get the terms of your lending agreement in writing (i.e., what to do if the instrument gets damaged, for example).

Please don't
Some schools have instruments for all of their first-year band members, and they may specifically ask you not to buy your child an instrument. Having the students play a school-owned instrument allows for instrument changes throughout the first year, initiated either by the school or your child. Has your child had a favorite instrument since long before being able to join the school program? Then you may of course consider purchasing an instrument and finding your youngster a private teacher.

Expensive instruments & low incomes
Other schools lend or rent the more expensive instruments only, such as bassoons, double basses, baritone saxophones, or tubas, and there are schools that loan a wide variety of instruments to families who can't afford them.

RENTING OR LEASING
Some schools and many music stores have rental instruments available on lease plans. Schools usually charge very low (often nominal) fees.

Return or sell
Renting or leasing an instrument from a music store will be more expensive in the long run than buying one (just as it is with cars or other products of high value). The main advantage of renting or leasing is that you can simply return the instrument if your child decides to quit; whereas if you'd purchased it, you'd have to resell it, which isn't always easy to do. Tip: Some rental and lease plans allow your child to transfer between instruments.

Maintenance and insurance

Maintenance is usually included in the rental fee, but some plans offer it as a separate expense. The main thing is to make sure you don't have to worry about it. Insurance may be included as well. Make sure you understand what is and isn't covered under your lease or rental plan.

Fractional instruments

For violins and the other orchestral string instruments that

1/16
(8.5"/216 mm)

1/8
(9.5"/241 mm)

1/4
(10.5"/267 mm)

1/2
(11.5"/292 mm)

nut

bridge

3/4 (12.25" /311 mm)   **7/8** (12.75"/323 mm)   **4/4** (13"/330 mm)

The most popular violin sizes and their average string lengths, measured from nut to bridge. (Exact string lengths vary per maker.) As you can see, a ¹/₂ violin is not really 'half' as big as a ⁴/₄ model.

come in fractional sizes, there's another advantage renting rather then buying: Children will need a larger-sized instrument as they grow. Most of these plans provide children with a size-up as soon as it's necessary. You should only consider purchasing a full-sized instrument once your child is physically ready. For most children, this is around the age of twelve to fourteen.

More small instruments
There are also fractional guitars, as well as many other instruments that come in down-sized versions for young children (see pages 126–133). For such instruments, renting or leasing usually makes more sense than buying.

The basics
It is impossible to provide a detailed description of the infinite amount of different plans, terms, and conditions you will likely encounter when you decide to lease or rent an instrument. But here are the basics:
- Many rental plans are actually **rent-to-own plans**: The instrument is yours once the periodic payments you've made equals the list price. Note that this list price will usually be higher than what you would have paid had you just bought the instrument outright — which explains why most of these plans are interest free. The profit is in the difference between the standard, discounted street, or 'going' price, and the list price.
- Most of these rent-to-own or **hire-purchase plans** also have an option to buy the instrument before you're fully paid up; if you choose to buy the instrument, your rent paid to date will usually be applied to the instrument.
- With a **lease plan** — also known as a straight rental plan or rent-to-rent plan — you simply keep paying rent until you return the instrument. Rates are usually lower on these plans than those of rent-to-own plans. With these plans, renting for a long period of time will be, of course, more expensive than buying the instrument.

Tips
These tips and questions may help you decide between buying, renting, and leasing.
- Check the **going price** of the instrument you plan to rent or lease, and calculate how long you would need to

rent or lease it at that price. You don't want to end up paying twice an instrument's price and still not own it.

- Does the **fee** include instrument set-up, maintenance, finance or bank charges, and delivery to your home or your child's school? If not, how much extra will these things cost?
- Is **insurance** included, and if so, does it cover damage, theft, and loss?
- Is there a school **pickup service** for instruments that need repair?
- Do you get a **replacement instrument** if yours needs maintenance?
- Do you have to pay an **origination fee**, an application fee, or a deposit? These costs are usually non-refundable; they often may be applied to the rental, however.
- Is there a r**econditioning fee**, a stocking fee, or a depreciation fee when you return the instrument?
- See if the plan allows your child to **switch instruments**, either within the same family (e.g., from one stringed instrument to another) or of another family (e.g., from guitar to saxophone).
- Are you sure you're not **obliged to buy** the instrument at the end of the plan?
- Find out if you're allowed to buy the instrument **at any time** (referred to as 'buying out the contract'), and what the financial conditions to do so are. A store may offer you a discount on the unpaid balance, or apply a percentage of your paid-up rent to the price of the instrument (List price or street price? Check!) Percentages vary from store to store, typically anywhere from thirty to fifty percent.
- Can the rent you've paid to date also be applied towards **another instrument** (of the same or another family) than the one you contracted to rent?
- Some stores rent instruments on a **month-to-month basis**; others have a three-month minimum, and some rent instruments per semester or school year.
- If the instrument is rented on a school-year basis, what about the **summer holidays**? There are lenders that offer rent-free summer months if you sign up to rent for the upcoming school year.
- What about a **discount** if you rent two or three instruments from the same store?

• Final tip: Always read the **fine print**, and ask around
  before you decide.

Buy back

As an alternative to renting, some stores have a buy-back
option. If you return the instrument within a specified
period of time, the store buys it back for a percentage of
the original purchase price (e.g., 70% within six months,
50% within two years, and so on). Tip: The purchase price
is often lower than what you'd end up paying over the term
of a rental plan. Another tip: Buy-back plans may allow you
to switch to another type or higher quality instrument.

New or pre-rented

Most rented or leased orchestral string instruments will
be re-rentals (a.k.a. 'pre-rented instruments') because of
reasons mentioned earlier. For most other instruments,
you'll probably be offered the choice between new and
used. Some stores charge a lower rental fee for used instruments (this may vary from less than thirty to more than
fifty percent); others charge the same fee, but you pay less
when you decide to buy the instrument.

Rental fees

The amount of the rental fee will depend on the price and
quality of instrument, the services included (insurance,
maintenance, etc.), the finance charge and fees, and so on.
As a guideline, you'll pay some twenty to thirty dollars per
month for a student-line violin, viola, trumpet, or clarinet.
More expensive instruments will have a higher rental price,
of course. For example, rental fees for a tenor saxophone
or oboe may vary from thirty dollars for a used student-
line instrument, to ninety dollars for a higher quality new
one.

School rental fees

School rental fees are much lower, of course. You may be
able to rent an expensive instrument, such as a bassoon,
for less than fifty dollars per school year. Many schools
provide expensive instruments only (the ones you'd not
likely buy yourself), or they offer a limited number of
instruments of all kinds for families that can't afford to
buy or rent elsewhere.

BUYING

Buying an instrument outright is cheaper than renting one in the long run. It also shows children that you believe in their musical goals; and actually owning an instrument may be a great motivator for your child.

Discounts

Stores have different ways to make buying attractive. In addition to a buy-back plan , you may be offered a discount if you buy outright, or an even bigger discount if you pay with cash or a check rather than credit. Just like any other store, music stores also have special offers, sales, and so on; instruments and accessories are often offered below their suggested retail prices. And of course, music stores also sell music books, accessories and all kinds of gadgets that can make playing more fun (and that make great gifts for your child).

Music stores

Basically, there are three types of music stores:

- **Large chain stores** have lots of instruments on display and in stock. They often have soundproof rooms for trying out instruments, as well as other services. These stores either focus on combo instruments (acoustic, electric, and guitars, drums, keyboards, and so on) or they have a large range of band and/or orchestral instruments as well.

- **Local music stores**, often family-owned, usually have a smaller stock — which can actually make choosing an instrument much easier. Service is typically more personal, which adds value to the cost of their instruments, since they usually (!) can't beat the prices of chain stores. Most local music stores are so-called 'full-line' stores, carrying a wide variety of instruments. The general focus is on low- and medium-budget products.

- **Specialty stores** sell only instruments of a particular musical family or group of related families: drums guitars, strings, woodwinds, pianos, and so on. These types of stores typically offer both specialized information and instruments in a wide range of prices. Violin makers (a.k.a. *luthiers*) may also sell and rent student-line violins, violas, cellos, and double basses.

Internet and mail order

You can also buy musical instruments and accessories via the Internet or mail order — a great option if there are no music stores in your area. Internet and mail-order stores may be able to offer very attractive pricing as their operating costs are lower due to low overhead. However, they can't offer one-on-one personal service nor advise you on your favorite instrument, strings, sticks, heads, and other accessories (other than by phone), and you can't just walk in for instrument repair (it can, however, be shipped, which takes time and money, while many of these 'problems' can be solved in a minute if you get a knowledgeable in-store salesperson to take a look). Also, you can't play and compare instruments before buying, and this remains the best way to decide which guitar, saxophone, or violin is best for you.

That said, you can usually return an instrument you don't like within a certain period of time and get your money back.

Mainstream retailers

A growing number of mainstream or general retailers also sell musical instruments. Their prices are often very low, typically because the quality of the products is also low. You won't likely be able to consult knowledgeable salespeople, and trying the instrument out is usually not an option. If the instrument needs to be repaired or adjusted, you'll have to take it to a music store, where they may refuse to repair it because of reasons covered on page 101.

Which store?

The more instruments a store has on display, the harder it will be for you to choose among them. On the other hand, as selecting an instrument is mostly a matter of comparison, a wide selection gives you a greater basis on which to make your decision. It's important to find a store with salespeople who clearly enjoy their work and know what they're talking about. Tip: Ask friends, family, and your child's music teacher for suggestions on which music stores in the area you might visit (note that some organizations do not allow their teachers to give such advice). Some other things to look at:

• Is there an **in-house repair shop**?

- Do you get a **replacement instrument** if yours needs maintenance?
- Do they stock **method books** and other educational materials, or will they order them for you?
- Does the store offer private and/or group **lessons**?
- Do you get help and advice on **assembly**, **tuning**, and **maintenance** of the instrument?
- Is **parking** easy and inexpensive?

Expert ears

No two guitars are exactly alike, even if they're of the same brand and style — and that goes for all instruments with the exception of digital models, such as keyboards. There may be subtle differences in timbre (e.g., one violin sounds a tad darker than the other), which isn't of real importance for beginner's instruments; but out of ten 'identical' saxophones, one or more may play a little easier, or be better in tune than the others — and that's something your child will appreciate. Making such comparisons requires a good player, so if you don't play the instrument yourself, try to bring along someone who does. If that's not possible, visit a store with salespeople on staff who can play the instruments for you.

NEW OR SECONDHAND?

Most musical instruments last for a long time, and you can often buy a used intermediate-quality instrument for what you would have paid for a new student model. Buying second-hand usually does take more time, effort, and expertise, however.

Privately or in a store?

Purchasing a used instrument from a private party may be cheaper than buying the same one from a store. One of the advantages of buying a used instrument from a retailer, however, is that you can go back if you have questions or problems. Chances are the instrument has been checked and adjusted before being sold to you, and the store may offer you a limited warranty to back its dependability. Also, you may be able to choose between a number of models in stock, and in some cases you can even exchange the instrument you bought for a different one within a certain period of time. A good dealer will sell at a competitive price, whereas private sellers might ask way too much — either because they don't know any better, or because they think that you don't.

An expert

Bringing along an experienced player is even more important if you're buying second-hand from a private party. Without their expert advice, you might turn down a shoddy-looking but otherwise valuable instrument, or get saddled with one that looks great but doesn't sound or play well. Tip: A used five-hundred dollar instrument could easily require an additional five-hundred dollars or more in repairs before it can be played. Another tip: If you want to be sure you're not paying too much, get the instrument appraised first. An expert technician or sales-person can tell you what it's worth, whether it needs any work done, and what that work should cost you. If the seller is unwilling to allow an appraisal, that could be a warning sign of serious problems.

Internet?

The Internet is a great source for used gear, but buying a musical instrument that you haven't seen or heard could prove hazardous. You could luck out and find a great instrument for far below its market value, but you could just as easily end up paying lots of money for an unplayable piece of equipment.

Age

Is it important to know the age of a used instrument? That depends on the type of instrument. For many instruments, age doesn't really make a difference in terms of sound, intonation, or playability, as long as they're in good shape. Violins can last for hundreds of years (and often become worth much more as they get older!); pianos typically last fifty years or more; drums and guitars can still be in mint condition after dozens of years. Older saxophones and other wind instruments often don't play as well as newer instruments. Also, pre-World War II wind instruments may have a deviant standard tuning, rendering them useless for ensemble work with modern horns. Digital instruments such as keyboards and digital pianos become obsolete faster than most acoustic instruments as sounds, connections, and options continue to improve and expand (much like cell phones and cameras). Although they may be out-of-date, they're still playable, of course, and you may be able to get buy last year's still-great model for relatively little money! For more details and technical tips on buying second-hand instruments, please consult your relevant Tipbook (see page 191–195).

Paperwork
If you do buy second-hand, ask the sellers for any associated documents they might have: the original receipt, the manual, a brochure, and so on. These things may be fun to read, and helpful if you decide to resell the instrument. Also, find out if and when the instrument has had any professional checkups and maintenance. For pianos, this should include tuning; a piano that hasn't been tuned for years may become very hard or impossible to tune.

Stepping up
If your child is ready to move on to a better instrument, you may try to trade in the old one, sell it privately (this may be more profitable, but also more work), or keep it as a spare. Tip: Most wind instruments deteriorate rather quickly when they're not played and maintained.

ADDITIONAL COSTS
Apart from lesson fees and the rent or purchase of an instrument, there are some additional costs that you need to be aware of, ranging from sticks and strings to maintenance and tuning, band fees, and sheet music. Below are some examples. More details can be found in Tipbooks on the various instruments shown on pages 191–195. Music stands, metronomes, and tuners were discussed on pages 72–73.

Strings, reeds, heads...
String instruments periodically need new strings. Guitar strings cost less than violin or cello strings, but the latter last (much) longer. Drummers need new drum heads and new drum sticks from time to time, and reed instruments require new reeds once in while. For beginners, most of

these costs will be reasonable: A ten-dollar set of guitar strings easily lasts a year; beginning drummers are unlikely to go through many pairs of sticks or a drum head every single day (although some hard-hitting pros do, at some five to ten dollars for a pair of sticks!); saxophone and clarinet reeds typically cost between a dollar and a half to three dollars each, and they may last anywhere from a couple of days or less up to a month or more. Bassoon and oboe reeds cost more, but last longer.

Maintenance

Costs for repairs and professional maintenance can be kept to a minimum by taking proper care of an instrument. Daily maintenance usually takes little time and even less money. In many cases, a cleaner and a cloth are all you need. Consult your child's teacher, your dealer, or a book on your instrument for instructions and tips.

Wind instruments

Clarinets, saxophones, and other woodwinds need an annual COA (Cleaning, Oiling, Adjustment), which typically costs some fifty to seventy-five dollars. A complete overhaul is required for both woodwinds and brasswinds once every few years — the frequency and cost dependent on how well the instrument is maintained and how frequently it is played. Daily maintenance requires a very small investment in one or more special brushes, oil, and cleaners.

Pianos

Pianos need to be tuned two to three times a year at some sixty to a hundred dollars for each tuning. More extensive maintenance (e.g., checking and adjusting the instrument's action and pedals) is less frequent.

String instruments

String instruments require some maintenance daily (basically cleaning with a dry cloth), and many string players have their instruments checked annually. Rosin cakes are cheap, starting at around three dollars, and last a long time. The hair of a string player's bow needs to be replaced every few years, which should be done only by a professional.

Drums and guitars

Drum sets and guitars can function properly for many years without any professional attendance. Most special cleaners are low-cost, and some household cleaners work fine too.

Cases and covers

Always find out if a case or cover is included in the price of your child's instrument. You can do without one as long as the instrument doesn't leave the house, but even so, such protection is critical to guarding your investment against dust, dirt, and damage.

Sheet music

Your investment in sheet music may go up as your child progresses, but for the first couple of years they'll be limited to the few books specified by their teachers — which usually cost about ten to twenty dollars per book; and most students spend several months studying one book.

Insurance

Your home owners' policy may or may not cover damage, loss, or theft of your musical instruments; check the fine print on yours. If the instrument leaves the house — albeit for a weekly lesson, a rehearsal, or a concert — you'll probably need additional insurance to cover it during such circumstances.

Band and orchestra fees

Bands and orchestras often charge a fee to cover the costs of uniforms, transportation, equipment, music, competition entry fees, operations, and so on. Annual fees typically run between twenty and one hundred dollars. There may be extra fees for summer camps or tours.

Exam fees

Exam fees vary from board to board, and higher-level exams are more expensive than beginner's exams. Prices range from around fifty dollars for the latter to a hundred or two hundred dollars for the highest (non-professional) grades. Fees for theory exams are usually lower — say, from around thirty to fifty dollars.

All in all?

The total annual cost of funding your budding musician depends on many things: instrument rental, lessons (usually the costliest element), and maintenance can easily add up to a thousand to fifteen hundred dollars per year. But you may end up paying less if you borrow an instrument and/or enroll your child in group lessons through school, for example; or expect to pay more if the route you choose includes a highly qualified teacher, a high-quality, high-maintenance instrument, and all kinds of additional fees. Note that you may be able to help out at band or orchestra events in lieu of your child's annual ensemble fees, and that there are financial aid options for families with demonstrated financial needs. School music teachers and band directors should be able to inform you where to go for information on this.

7. WHICH INSTRUMENT?

For many children, the question of which instrument to play is something they don't need to mull over — they already know. But what if your child doesn't? The following chapter looks at this topic from a number of different perspectives, and questions various preconceived ideas on instrument selection.

If children express a strong desire to play a certain instrument, you should probably trust their instincts — if their heart is in it, they'll be more motivated to stick with it. Conversely, playing the 'wrong' instrument is probably one of the main reasons that children quit their music programs or private lessons. In other words, the answer to the question, 'Which instrument?' can be of crucial importance to the longevity of your child's musical ambitions.

But...

That said, even children who passionately expressed a desire to play a certain instrument may give up after a couple of months; and kids who were assigned an instrument because it was the only one available could end up falling in love with it and becoming successful professionals. Still, if you want your children to enjoy playing music, you'll improve your (and their) chances by at least letting them have a say in choosing their instrument.

Sound and looks

Children often choose an instrument because they like its sound, its looks, or both. Exposing them to music — preferably live music in a wide variety of styles, including the ones you yourself might not like — allows them to identify instruments and develop a preference. Anything else you do to encourage your child musically, as discussed in Chapter 3, will help.

A friend

Children may also pick an instrument because a friend plays it and they want to join in, or because they're drawn to an artist who plays that particular instrument. Though you may worry that choosing by such criteria may not be sound or lasting, those are not the worst criteria for choosing either. The same goes for kids who want to join their friends' garage band and simply start playing the lacking instrument — be it bass, drums, or guitar.

Availability

Having instruments around the house can also inspire a child's desire. Many children start playing the piano or guitar just because they happen to be available. If they pick up the instrument of their own accord, rather than being pressured to play it because it's there, that's a good sign that the instrument is right for them, and that they'll likely be a motivated student.

Siblings

Younger children may be inspired by the instrument an older sibling plays. Some will argue that you should dissuade them from playing the same instrument in order to avoid sibling rivalry — but this is bound to happen anyway; it's just part of life. If the siblings have a good relationship, the older one can even help guide the younger one. And while the idea of a family ensemble might sound appealing, your children may not appreciate being assigned an instrument based solely on the musical needs of the ensemble that you have in mind.

Friends and relatives

Getting hands-on experience with different instruments can help you make a more informed choice. Ask friends and relatives who play — amateurs, professionals, and anyone in between — to demonstrate their instruments for your children. They might be willing to let them have a go at it too.

Exploratory courses

Some academic and music schools offer exploratory courses allowing children to try various instruments temporarily. By taking advantage of such courses, children may learn basic techniques and may even get to do some ensemble work that incorporates all the available instruments (preferably in different styles of music). This is probably the best option for children who want to play but are having difficulty making up their minds on an instrument. It's also a great way to open new horizons for kids who have already made their choice.

Guidance

Guiding your children as they choose their instruments requires little more than a bit of common sense. Some examples? If your child loves to sing, but also wants to play an instrument, the guitar or piano are good choices as both instruments can be played as vocal accompaniment. Solitary learners may like these instruments as well — but they can make them even more solitary…

Instruments and styles

Some instruments will unavoidably influence your child toward a certain musical style. The oboe and bassoon are hardly used outside the field of classical music, for instance, and some types of brasswinds are hardly seen outside of a wind band. So, for example, if your child has a deep love of classical music, you might want to suggest the clarinet over the saxophone, as there are fewer classical repertoires for this relatively young instrument.

That said, it's better to be open to what musical direction could be taken, rather than limiting your child to the directions that have been followed before. Ian Anderson's success as the flute player for the legendary rock band Jethro Tull is just one of the many examples of how instruments can be used in a non-traditional way.

Whatever instrument

For children who simply love being part of the band or school orchestra, the instrument choice may not matter that much; you might even suggest that they choose one of the instruments needed most. Even professional musicians sometimes take this route: If music is their livelihood, and playing the double bass just happens to be lucrative, they play the double bass...

Reading, writing, piano playing

Some parents simply make music lessons a non-debatable part of their children's upbringing. Just like their children have to go to school and learn reading, writing and arithmetic at one point, they require them to take piano lessons for one, two or three years, and then allow them to choose another instrument, or to quit. Learning piano provides a solid foundation for learning other instruments — so if you take this approach, the piano would be a good choice. But also remember it's not the only choice.

Switching instruments

No matter what the reason that children end up with whatever instrument they do, chances are they'll want to switch after a couple of years, or even sooner. Even adults tend to change their minds, and children are a lot more likely to develop new preferences, discover new sounds, or to just want to change because they *want* to... Young violinists may want to switch to the electric guitar when they get into their teens, for example, and forcing them to stick with violin may compel them to quit. But allowing them to explore the guitar could enrich their musical education as well.

Within the same family

However, a child cannot effectively progress if he or she is switching instruments every year. If your child ends up not liking the instrument they chose, first suggest that they switch to an instrument within the same family (from flute to saxophone, rather than guitar, for example), so much of what they've already learned can be applied to the new instrument. Chances are, however, that children who have grown to really dislike a woodwind won't want to choose an instrument from that same family.

Failure or success

Many well-known musicians switched instruments when they were younger — some because they liked another instrument better; others because they had trouble learning their first instrument (such as the well-known drummer who started on cello but was made to stop because he couldn't count!). This also addresses the concern that you can't succeed on one instrument if you failed on another — you most certainly can.

Success

Desire is one of the best motivators. A child who desires to play a certain instrument will usually succeed at it, especially if success is measured in terms of enjoyment and the motivation to persist, rather than in terms of reaching a certain standard. So even if it seems as though the odds are against your child's instrument choice, it's usually best to give in and let their desires prevail. But what if your child has genuine limitations? For example, can you learn to play the trumpet with a harelip and cleft palate? Although perhaps not the easiest of endeavors, there's a least one professional trumpeter who did, simply because he wanted to. (There's more on the physical aspects of choosing an instrument on page 123–126.)

ASSIGNING INSTRUMENTS

Band directors need a certain number of each instrument for a full ensemble, and instrument assignment for school bands and orchestras can be more about matching students to the required instruments (after all, you can't have a wind band with twelve drummers and two clarinetists) than about what the student may prefer.

Tests

Some schools use aptitude tests to determine which instrument would be best for your child. These tests are often followed by a (classroom of individual) demonstration of the various instruments for students and their parents. Some schools ask the students to choose their top three favorite instruments from the band's line up, and then assign them one of the three.

Even teeth, pointed chin

Matching student to instrument is a skill that necessitates a great deal of attentiveness to the student and his or her needs. It's definitely not as simple as the lists that assess physical attributes suggest: "Even teeth, a pointed chin, and medium lips? A clarinetist. Same features but a round chin? That's a trombone player." There's more on this on page 123–126.

Grades

Some schools select particular students for 'difficult' instruments (typically the oboe, bassoon, and French horn) because they get good grades. However, there doesn't seem to be any evidence of a relationship between academic performance and one's talent for these — or any other — instruments. Other schools make the 'popular' instruments available only to students with the highest scores as a way of limiting the number of applicants, or they prohibit certain instruments from students with histories of academic or behavioral problems. As a parent, it is good to be aware of such rules.

TALENTS AND ABILITIES

If children really want to play an instrument, lack of talent or natural ability can usually be made up for in sheer desire — and ability may increase as they go. In other words, you can advise a kid with poor foot-hand coordination not to play the drums, but you could also see this as an opportunity for that child to improve this coordination — especially if that instrument is the one favored by the child. If you see your child putting in a lot of hard work without any success, you can always switch instruments. Some teachers may also suggest a different instrument if they feel that the switch would better benefit your child's specific talents, motor skills, or musical preference. If you present the proposed switch to your child as something that he or she will benefit from, the answer will probably be yes.

Relative pitch

All children have the ability to develop a musical ear, to some degree at least. And you can definitely improve your *relative pitch*, which enables you to hear whether you're playing in tune or not. This skill is important for everyone who plays an instrument that requires you to control the exact pitch yourself — from orchestral strings to brass-winds and woodwinds — and for all players who tune their own instruments. Even drummers need a sense of pitch if they want to make their drums sound perfect!

Absolute pitch

Whether you can actually be trained in or develop *perfect pitch* or *absolute pitch* (the ability to recognize and name a pitch without any reference) is debatable. People who have perfect pitch aren't always glad they do — it's horrible if you have to play a piano that's just below or above standard tuning, for example.

PHYSICAL FEATURES

Should trumpeters have thin lips? Not really: Just look at trumpeter Wynton Marsalis or his late fellow players, Louis Armstrong and Dizzy Gillespie. Should violin players have medium-sized hands? Not really. Some great violinists have small hands, some large; some lean fingers, some stocky. Some great double bassists have small hands.

All shapes and sizes

Selecting an instrument based on the potential player's physique is a hazardous affair; you can't measure people and tell them what to play based on that assessment. Though it is undeniably true that certain physical features can make certain instruments a bit easier or harder to play, it is also true that a kid's desire to play a certain instrument can overcome almost all of their physical, and other, features and characteristics. One look at the violin section of a symphony orchestra is enough to tell you that violinists come in all shapes and sizes, and the same goes for all other instrumentalists.

Aware

Still, it's good to know that some physical characteristics could get in the way or slow your child down. Teachers and band directors are usually aware of such factors and will pinpoint, and perhaps solve, the problem before the child gets too discouraged and quits (the real reason possibly unknown to them or you). Below are some random thoughts and facts on the subject.

Lips

Lips are mainly important for brasswind players and flutists.
- The size of your lips has no impact on your ability to play larger or smaller brasswinds. The texture of your lips does,

to some extent, but this kind of determination should be left to a professional: Soft, supple lips can make playing brasswind instruments with large mouthpieces easier to play, while tougher lips may be easier for trumpeters.

- All brasswinds require that your lips meet properly, so you can create the lip valve (a.k.a. 'lip reed') you need to generate sound. A short upper lip is no problem as long as it's compensated for by a longer lower lip, for example.

- To enjoy playing a brasswind instrument, you need a mouthpiece that suits your physique. Given the right mouthpiece, you can basically play any brass instrument regardless of your type of lips. Trying nothing but a standard mouthpiece may steer talented students away from instruments they really like.

- Flutists depend on their lips too, and much has been said regarding lip shapes that make playing this instrument hard, or even impossible. However, with enough attention, a good teacher, and a motivated student, most of these and many other 'problems' can be overcome rather easily. For example, a teardrop-shaped upper lip splits the flutist's air column, which can be a problem, but changing the relative position of the lips — rolling the upper lip out, or simply repositioning the flute — may be enough to solve this issue.

Teeth

The shape and size of a child's teeth can play a role too, but again, it's always best to let children have a go at the instrument they want to play. Some kids with irregular and large front teeth play the flute effortlessly, while another kid with 'perfect flute teeth' may not be able to produce even the faintest sound on the instrument.

- Chapter 3 discussed the influence of braces and whether it's important to have your permanent teeth before playing a wind instrument; see pages 51–55.

- For flutists, a gap between the front teeth can cause loss of pressure. A dentist can adjust the gap.

- A profound underbite or overbite can make playing a wind instrument quite hard. Choosing the right mouthpiece can help alleviate this problem for brass players. The same goes for saxophonists and clarinetists, and there are all kind of special head joints for flutists available.

Lefties

Left-handed players can play any instrument a right-handed player can, and most instruments do not come in 'left-handed' editions. Some do — but there's a usually a but:

- Left-handed guitars and bass guitars are available — but in smaller numbers than right-handed instruments, and they're often more expensive.
- Left-handed drummers and Latin percussionists can simply re-arrange their instrument to accommodate themselves — but this makes using someone else's set, including their teacher's, harder or even impossible.
- At a price, orchestral string instruments can be adapted — but players who play 'the wrong way around' may not be welcome in an orchestra, simply because of the visual aspect.
- A few 'left-handed' pianos have been made — but their owners will only be able to play that one instrument, which is a serious handicap as they can't take it along…

Double-jointed fingers

Children with double-jointed fingers (joint laxity, or hypermobility) may have problems with certain instruments (*e.g.*, guitar, piano, flute, oboe). Special exercises and proper guidance and advice from a dedicated, knowledgeable teacher often helps. Also, professional players with hypermobility suffer less from aches and pains than those without this condition!

Respiratory problems

You may think that children with respiratory problems should not play a wind instrument, but the fact is that they can actually benefit from such practice. For example, quite a number of professional wind players were advised to play their instrument *because* they had asthma.

Physical impairments

There are specialists who can adapt instruments to a wide variety of physical impairments — special guitar stands, one-of-a-kind wind instruments for players with a missing hand or missing fingers, and vertical or 'swan neck' flutes for children whose disability prevents them from holding a regular flute properly. Tip: The trumpet is one of the very few instruments that can be played with one hand without adaptations. Another tip: Using the 'full keyboard' mode on a home keyboard allows a single-handed player to play both the accompaniment and the melody or a solo! For more information on these and many other solutions, you may consult specialized instrument makers or the organizations on page 188.

An ergonomically adapted 'swan neck' flute (Flutelab).

Size

When it comes to physical size, most kids are capable of playing any instrument by ten or eleven years of age (about fifth grade), which is the age most school bands and orchestras begin recruiting. For younger kids, there are various special smaller-sized instruments available (see below) and some instruments can simply be adapted to their size — so they don't need long arms to play the trombone, or be a giant to start playing the double bass. Many small adults also play down-sized instruments, from short scale bass guitars and Concert-type steel-string guitars to ⅞ violins. A full-sized double bass is too big for most adult bass players; they usually play a ¾ size.

DOWN-SIZED INSTRUMENTS AND AGES

Why do kids as young as four often start on the violin? Because it's one of the few instruments available in such small sizes. There are also fractional violas and cellos for kids this age, as covered on page 105. Most other down-sized instruments are still a bit too big for kids this young. Below are some of the better and lesser-known examples. Guidelines on the age at which children could start playing various instruments are included. But keep in mind that they're no more than suggestions, really: Your eight-year-old may be bigger than the neighbor's ten-year-old. Please note that some of the instruments listed below may not (yet) be available in your country.

Wind instruments

The sooner you begin on your instrument, the better. The main reason kids can't start playing most of the wind instruments until around the age of six or seven is because these instruments are too big and heavy. Kids need wind instruments that are lightweight, easy to play, and possibly feature fewer keys than the 'adult' versions. Unfortunately, the number of down-sized wind instruments is still quite limited, and these perfectly viable instruments are currently made by small companies only. Even though numerous kids enjoy these instruments very much (they don't have to wait to play the oboe until they're eleven anymore!), not all teachers are fully convinced of their value. This may not change until the leading makers of larger wind instruments start producing down-sized versions, allowing them to gain wider acceptance.

Supports and harnesses

Tip: Neck straps and harnesses are available for making wind instruments easier to play for young children (and for adults, too!). However, because they don't reduce the weight, but rather redistribute it, these instruments may still be too heavy for your child.

Recorder

There's an instrument that needs no down-sizing: the recorder. Children can play this instrument as soon as they are capable of closing all the toneholes, which is typically when they're five or six. The recorder is also very affordable (forty or fifty dollars can get you a good instrument); it hardly needs maintenance, and a child can learn to play a few simple songs in no time. Playing the recorder also helps develop the fine motor skills you need to play any other instrument, and it can be played alone, in recorder ensembles, or accompanied by a piano, for example. Being a relatively 'easy' instrument, children can focus on learning to read music as they play the recorder, experiencing how written notes translate to pitches. For these and other reasons, the recorder is often considered a great instrument for all budding musicians, and especially for aspiring woodwind players. However, children who are old and big enough are usually better off starting right away with the instrument of their choice. The fingering of the recorder vaguely resembles that required for other woodwinds, but fingering is a relatively easy thing to learn. Also, all other woodwinds demand a very different *embouchure* (how to use the muscles in and around your mouth to blow the instrument).

Flute

Though relatively light and small, a flute is not the easiest instrument to hold. A number of flute makers produce special junior models that feature offset finger buttons and extended keys that decrease the wide spacing of the regular instrument's keys, while a curved head joint brings all levers and keys closer to the player. Some teachers dislike flutes with curved head joints because they can lead to bad posture. Also, balancing the instrument is said to become a little harder. As the curved head joint leaves little room to grab the instrument by its non-keyed parts, assembling the instrument is a bit harder too. Alternatively, teachers have children start on very affordable, plastic keyless flutes, or on the E♭ flute, which is a little smaller than the regular concert flute. Student models of this particular flute are not as common as regular student flutes, however. The piccolo, the

A keyless plastic flute and a children's flute.

flute family's smallest member, is not suited for beginning players as it's not only harder to play; it's also harder to play in tune.

Saxophone

Most beginning saxophone players start on alto saxophone when they're around ten years of age. At that age, the larger tenor is usually too big and too heavy, and the smaller soprano and sopranino saxophones are much harder to play. If the alto is still too big, aspiring sax players are usually advised to start on clarinet, a different, yet very similar instrument with the same type of mouthpiece. Switching from the clarinet to the saxophone is easier than the other way around.

Clarinet

Most teachers advise children not to start the clarinet before they're eight to ten years of age. Some companies make special clarinets for younger children, such as the Kinderklari and the Lyons clarinets. The latter, designed for children from age five or six, weighs about one-third that of a regular clarinet, has a simplified mechanism, is more durable, and needs less maintenance. Not all teachers endorse these instruments, but if your youngster loves the sound of the clarinet, find a teacher who does — they're the ones who don't believe in asking a child to wait for a couple years. Tip: Some private teachers have younger kids start on the E♭ clarinet: a smaller, higher pitched voice of the flute family. The choice of student models of regular B♭ clarinets is much bigger, though.

Saxonett

The Saxonett is a child's instrument designed for aspiring clarinet and saxophone players, consisting of a wooden, recorder-like body without keys, and a clarinet mouthpiece.

Oboe

Many kids start on the oboe when they're nine to eleven years of age. Their first instrument is

The Lyons clarinet.

A children's
oboe
(Guntram Wolf,
Germany).

usually a plastic one, which weighs less than a wooden oboe. A light reed makes the instrument easier to play. Kids can start playing oboes at a much earlier age, however: A German company makes oboes with few keys, and even without keys, that can be played by children from age six or even younger.

Bassoon
The bassoon is a large instrument that requires quite a large hand span to play. You're big enough to play the bassoon once you're the same size as the instrument, which is typically around the age of ten or eleven. For smaller kids, various companies offer bassoons with a covered C-hole. Bassoon makers can also adapt the instrument to smaller hands, but this doesn't reduce the weight of the instrument. The aforementioned German company also produces a down-sized bassoon that can be played by six-year-olds.

Trumpet
There are piccolo trumpets, but they're not meant for children. Many eight- or nine-year-olds start on the cornet, an instrument that is very similar to the trumpet. It's easier to handle because it's a bit shorter, and easier to play because it requires less air pressure. The even shorter and easier-blown flugelhorn can be offered as an alternative for young kids too.

Trombone
There are various options for seven- to nine-year-olds who want to play the trombone:
- An **alto trombone** is a bit smaller and lighter than the regular-sized (tenor) trombone.
- A tenor trombone can be fitted with an **extension arm** that allows students with shorter arms to reach the 6th and 7th positions. However, the instrument is still very large and hard to balance if you're small.
- Some companies make special junior or

compact trombones with **shorter slides** and other adaptations.

- The Quadro is a trombone with a slide made up of **four short tubes** instead of two long ones, so even small children can reach the 6th and 7th positions. The extremely short slide also facilitates intricate maneuvers for marching band members.

The Quadro trombone.

French horn

The French horn basically comes in two versions: the single horn, tuned either in B♭ or in F, and the double horn, which can be shifted from B♭ to F with an extra valve. Most players start on a single horn, usually switching to the double horn after one or two years of playing. A few companies make a French horn for children, which is a bit lighter and has a special type of wrap that makes it smaller and thus easier to handle.

Baritone, tenor horn, tuba

Most other brasswinds (e.g., *background brass instruments* such as the baritone, tenor horn, or tuba) can be played by most kids at age eight or nine. Aspiring tuba players usually start on a smaller background brass instrument, and they can usually switch to tuba around the age of eleven or twelve. Tip: There are ¾ tubas for smaller players.

Guitar

Acoustic guitars are available in various fractional sizes; the smallest is typically around three-quarters the size of a standard instrument. (There is no consensus on how to indicate this size. Some companies call it a ½ guitar, others ⅛, or ¼.) Most smaller guitars have nylon strings, but there are down-sized steel-string ('folk') guitars too, as well as down-sized electric guitars that can be played by most kids around the age of seven. Kids who fall in love with the instrument at an even younger age may start on a ukulele, a four-string Hawaiian family member.

Percussion
Percussion instruments are very accessible; all you have to do is hit or shake them (although playing them musically requires a lot more than that!). This explains why there are so many small percussion instruments for children: from frame drums in all sizes and shapes, to shakers and bongos, tambourines, and xylophones. The choice is yours.

Drums
Toy drum sets should not be confused with higher quality down-sized drum sets, which your child will enjoy much more. Visit a music store for the real thing. Note that junior drum sticks are also available — regular sticks are way too heavy and too large for young players.

Piano and keyboard
The piano is a great instrument to start on. You watch your hands as you play, all the keys are neatly arranged from the low notes on your left to the high notes on your right, and it's the ideal tool for developing a foundational understanding of music and therefore the perfect instrument to start on before moving on to another. Being a virtual orchestra on its own, it is used by numerous composers of many styles, and many musicians play it as their secondary instrument. Even though a regular piano keyboard is quite large for most kids' hands, many children start playing this instrument at a very early age — some as young as three or four. The main thing is to find a teacher who wants to teach your child at such a young age. Toy pianos come in all shapes and colors, but they're toys, not pianos. The same basically goes for digital home keyboards with down-sized keys.

Harp
As the pedal harp is such an expensive instrument, with prices typically starting around ten thousand dollars, children tend to start with smaller types of harps, such as the Celtic harp (a.k.a. 'lever harp' or 'folk harp'). It typically

features between thirty-one and forty strings. Celtic harps can be played by most six-year olds, but they're played by adults too. There are smaller harps for even younger kids.

Accordion
The accordion, known as the poor man's piano until the advent of the home keyboard, is another instrument available in various junior sizes. Again, do note the difference between toy instruments and the real thing. A toy is something you can only play with; an instrument is something you play.

Double bass
Most seven-year-olds can start on a ⅛ or ¹⁄₁₀ double bass. These instruments are some sixteen inches shorter than a regular, adult ¾ double bass (see page 126). Is your child younger than seven? There are four-year-olds playing 'bass' on a ⅛ cello with adapted strings that allow for a bass tuning!

Making instruments more accessible
There are many ways that teachers can make instruments more accessible to young children. For example, they may use colored stickers on the fingerboard of a violin (indicating the correct positions). Similar stickers can be used for guitar or ukulele (put your fingers on the blue stickers to play a G-major chord!). Some use colored stickers on the keys of a piano or a home keyboard to correspond with notation in those same colors. At the same time, other teachers put stickers on the bars of bell sets, which usually have the note names engraved: Hiding these letters helps the student learn to recognize the positions of the bars, rather than reading their note names.

GENDER
Even though the number of female drummers, bassists, electric guitarists, and trombonists has increased over the years, children still tend to think of these instruments as being 'for boys.' Likewise, the flute and harp are among the instruments still considered to be 'for girls.' Needless to say, gender should not play a role when it comes to choosing an instrument. Hopefully, the fact that violins, guitars, and

other instruments with a fingerboard require clipped nails to effectively stop the strings never kept anyone from choosing such an instrument.

PERSONALITY

It is true that the typical flutist tends to possess a character different than the typical percussionist (assuming that 'typical' flutists and percussionists even exist). Also, there may be significant differences in the temperaments of trumpeters versus oboists. However, when it comes to choosing instruments, children's personalities should be about as important as the way they look or dress — literally, that is. There are enough kids with pierced eyebrows who love playing Mahler to prove this. There are drummers who are sweet and gentle, just as there are bassists (you know, the silent people in the back of the band) with the personality and authority of a sledgehammer. So suggesting that physical or 'aggressive' kids to play 'physical' instruments is probably not as good an idea as suggesting that they join the marching band rather than the orchestra — but maybe they'd be even better off if they *would* join the orchestra, and then play ball or go boxing to balance things out...

EASY INSTRUMENTS?   Tipcode KIDS-003

The piano is one of the easiest instruments to play a scale on: Just press eight white keys in a row, one after the other, and you're done. But is the piano an easy instrument? No. There are no easy instruments, actually. It's just that some instruments are a bit easier to start on. For most kids, the flute is easier to start on than the oboe, though some never get a flute to sound any good. Brass instrumentalists often have a slower start than saxophonists, even though a saxophone with all its keys looks far more complex. The saxophone's key mechanism actually makes producing different notes a lot easier than that of a brass instrument. Because the latter only has three 'keys,' it requires that you develop your embouchure to produce all the notes in a scale.

Difficulties

Each instrument has its own difficulties or challenges. The

piano requires that you play two parts at the same time, and often one or both hands press more than one key simultaneously (chords). Organ players also use their left foot for the bass parts, and often their right to control their volume. The left hand of a violinist or a classical guitarist does something completely different from their right. Drummers need to develop four-way coordination, using their four limbs simultaneously. And so on…

Rock musicians
Numerous amateur rock guitarists, bassists, and drummers master their instruments to a point where they can perform successfully in a matter of months. By that time they're all set to have tons of fun for years to come. That doesn't make their instruments easy to play, however. It's just that most rock (and country, folk, etc.) songs can be played without being a virtuoso musician. This is not to say that there are no virtuoso rock, country, and folk musicians — of course, there are.

The singing voice
The most accessible musical instrument is the singing voice, and the easiest way to be musically active without having to practice daily is to join a choir — a school choir, a church choir, a pop choir, or any other type of choir (although if you really want to learn how to sing, you can't do so without a voice teacher or a vocal coach; and many singers do practice daily).

Percussion
Percussion instruments offer instant gratification; you can join a drum circle without any previous experience (but there are percussionists who can play a flabbergasting, fascinating five-minute solo on no more than a tambourine, and it took them years of practice).

Keyboard
Home keyboards have built-in, umpteen-piece band or orchestra options that play fully automated beginnings and endings to your songs, in any style you want, while creating the most complex chords at the push of a button (but there are virtuoso keyboard players who can make each built-in digital sound like a real instrument).

More?

All the instruments detailed above are no more than a few examples of those that offer a relatively easy start. And of course, what a child finds to be 'easy' or 'hard' depends on the child as much as on the instrument. If your child doesn't seem to be making a connection with the instrument of his or her choice, switching instruments may solve things. But first, make sure that their original instrument is in good shape, as discussed on page 100; don't let a deficient instrument cause your child to feel erroneously incompetent and quit.

NOISE, SIZE, PRICE

The number of decibels and contact sound an instrument produces might be a consideration when it comes to choosing an instrument. So might size. Can your kid carry the instrument to school or to lessons, or do they need a car to transport it? Do you have room for an acoustic piano or a drum set, and can it be played without bothering the neighbors? (Though the latter problem can be solved by buying a digital piano or an electronic drum set — there's more on this on pages 75–80). Instrument prices can be a consideration as well: Harps, French horns, tubas, and baritone saxophones are more costly than guitars, trumpets, and home keyboards. Your child's school may loan or rent such expensive instruments at a nominal fee, or you can research instrument programs available in your area. The school's music teacher, the band director, or people at the local music store should be able to assist you.

MORE THAN ONE
Tipcode KIDS-004

Many musicians play more than one instrument: either one from the same instrument family, or a completely different one. Some examples:

- Various instruments are available in **different voices**, such as the saxophone, flute, or clarinet. If you play one of these, the other voices are relatively — sometimes very — easy to learn. (Still, most players favor one of those voices!)
- Many **sax players** double on the clarinet (and vice versa), or the flute.
- If you're a **trumpeter**, the cornet and the flugelhorn are

two instruments within easy technical reach. Switching between larger (background) brass instruments such as the tuba or the baritone is quite easy too. **French horn** and **trombone players** rarely choose to play another brasswind.

- Mastering a **keyboard** instrument is a great basis for learning and understanding all other instruments, and it gives you relatively easy access to all other keyboard instruments — even though an organ requires a different approach than a piano, for example.

- Some musicians also learn a second instrument to **broaden their scope**. If you play a melody instrument (trumpet, violin, oboe, etc.), you may opt for an instrument that allows you to play chords, or vice versa. And for musicians who're always in the back of the band, such as drummers and bassists, it can be an enlightening experience to learn how to play some of the melodies they're always backing up. The opposite is also true!

8. PLAYING TOGETHER

Making music, to most people, means making music together. And practicing, to many people, is something you do to learn an instrument so well that you can join a band, an orchestra, or other ensemble. Here's why playing in a group is so important, followed by an introduction to the main types of musical groups.

Listening to a solo cellist or trumpeter can be fun for a while, but it will be more interesting if they're playing in a band or an orchestra — and the same goes for most other instruments. Drummers and bassists need a band to back up, just like vocalists and soloists need to be backed up, and so on...

Solo?

A few instruments are more suited to playing solo, such as the home keyboard, the piano, and the acoustic guitar. Still, many guitarists prefer playing within some type of ensemble, and playing the piano is often more fun with others, too — joining a jazz quartet, accompanying a violinist, a flutist, or a choir.

Benefits

Some of the main benefits of making music with others were briefly mentioned in Chapter 1. Here are some additional thoughts.

First of all, playing in a group provides players with performance opportunities, which is a great motivator. What good is it to practice your oboe or your guitar every day if no one ever hears what you can do?

Fellow musicians

Even if your child's group does not yet perform, playing in a group can help inspire their practice. They need to be able to play their part so as to not to let their fellow musicians and the conductor down, which is a different concern than not performing well for their teacher.

Cooperative environment

Bands and orchestras provide your child with a cooperative environment where they learn to function in both smaller units (e.g., the viola section) and larger groups (the entire orchestra). They also learn how to respond to and take directives from an authority figure (the conductor or band director). The same goes for athletic activities, of course. What makes music different is that there's nobody to play against, which appeals to a different type of motivation. You don't have to be engaged in a competition to have a common goal. And for those who love the competitive element, there are plenty of competing bands!

Better musicians

Playing in a group makes children better musicians, opening their ears and their minds to all the elements that make up music.

Level

Children can usually join a school band or orchestra soon after they started playing, and they will usually find that their fellow musicians play at or around the same level as they do. If things are good, the better players in the group will inspire the newcomers, who will now have something tangible to aim for. However, big differences in playing levels can intimidate children rather than inspire them. Conversely, adept children may lose interest if they've surpassed their fellow band members. It may help if advanced players are assigned to a special position in the band, or if they're inspired to help 'lagging' players out. If not, finding another band may be the best solution.

No waiting

The sooner your child joins a group the better, for all the reasons mentioned above. However, if your child has been playing alone for a couple of years, no matter how adept, he or she may still feel a bit intimidated when they discover that the band won't wait for them when he or she makes a mistake or gets lost in the music. That said, being in a violin section or a brass section can be an inspiring and safe place. Hearing all the right notes around you makes it easier for you to play along (and you can often skip a few notes without anyone noticing…).

Being in the band

Playing in a group means dedicating extra time, both for you and your child. A weekly rehearsal (to which you may have to take your child) is probably the very least you can expect. Most bands and orchestras rehearse more than once a week, some do on every school day. And if there's an upcoming performance, they add another few hours.

Time management

Upcoming performances often demand a little extra time management. Make sure you know your child's workload (or make sure they know themselves); encourage them to work ahead on their school assignments so they'll have little to no homework to do on the day of the performance.

Seeking bands and orchestras...

If your child's school has no band or orchestra opportunities, consult your child's private instructor, your local recreation and community center, your state's art council, the community music school, or the band director of a nearby college. You can also check music stores' bulletin boards and the classified ads in musicians' magazines or your local newspaper, or search the Internet. For everyone who's looking for a band, there's a band looking for them. Tip: Many cities have one or more community orchestras and bands.

...or starting one

You or your child may also consider initiating an ensemble yourselves, with or without the assistance of other parents or students. The school may provide a rehearsal room, for example. Opportunities to make music with others can always be found or cultivated, though it may take time to locate people who play the instruments your ensemble is lacking, are at or around the same level of musicianship as the rest of the group, have an interest in playing the same style of music, and are willing to invest the necessary amount of time, and so on. But you don't have to go for a seventy piece wind symphony or a full-blown big band right-away: Playing in a guitar duo, a horn trio, a string quartet, or a jazz quintet will provide your child with most or all of the benefits of joining a larger group.

Audition
Some ensembles, orchestras, bands, and choirs may require applicants to audition before being invited to join. Auditions are usually divided into various parts, such as playing one or more prepared songs or sections, sight-reading, scales, and improvisation or solo playing. Tips on preparing for auditions are in Chapter 10.

TYPES OF BANDS, ORCHESTRAS AND OTHER GROUPS
Music is made by every combination of instruments and musicians you can imagine. There are violists who play with African percussionists, bassoonists who play jazz, opera singers who join rock groups, cellists who play heavy metal, and so on. It goes without saying that there is no clear-cut label for these combos, other than the general terms 'group' or 'ensemble.' Labels for traditional groups aren't exactly standardized or unambiguous either, as you will see on the following pages.

Bands and ensembles
The word 'band' can refer to a wide variety of musical groups: a four-piece funk group, a school's marching band, a big band (jazz), a one-hundred-piece wind band, a concert band… 'Ensemble,' the French word for 'together,' is another generic term. The word is often used for classical groups that have five or more members, but are still smaller than an orchestra.

Combinations of two, three, four, or five members are usually called duos, trios, quartets, and quintets respectively; those terms are common in the classical world, but also among jazz musicians, for example. Some also use the labels sextet (six musicians), septet (seven), octet, nonet, or even dectet.

Classification

It's impossible to create a textbook classification for the infinite variety of musical groups, if only because there are so many completely diverse types of groups playing the same style of music, and so many groups with very similar instrumentations playing very different styles of music. Below is a random tour of a number of popular types of ensembles, their instrumentation, and the music they typically play. Please refer to Chapter 9 for short descriptions of the instruments mentioned below and elsewhere in this book.

SCHOOL BANDS AND ORCHESTRAS

In the U.S., some types of ensembles are typically part of school, college, or university music programs, such as concert bands, marching bands, jazz bands, pep bands, and orchestra. Similar groups also exist outside of educational institutions.

Concert bands, symphonic winds

Concert band and *symphonic winds* are two of the many different names for a large, non-marching group of some forty to more than a hundred woodwind, brasswind, and percussion players. The repertoire can include classical music, ballads, musical comedy, jazz, sacred music, patriotic songs — and more. Other names for similar ensembles are *wind symphony*, *wind band*, *wind orchestra*, or *wind ensemble*. Because you will find that 'standard' instrumentation is used by these differently labeled bands, it's clear that these labels don't mean much. These ensembles typically incorporate French horns, baritones next to trumpets and trombones, clarinets and saxophones in various voices, flutes and oboes, and orchestral percussion. Other instruments may be added, such as a string section, or a string bass.

Same instrumentation, different level

Some schools have a concert band, a symphonic band, *and* a wind ensemble, for example. Since each of these groups include similar instrumentation and repertoire, their names typically imply either different levels of musicianship or that their members are of different age groups or grades.

Marching band

The marching band has its roots in the military, and its members' uniforms typically reflect that heritage. But instead of leading and inspiring the troops, today's marching bands play at sporting events — especially American football games — so they're also referred to as *athletic bands*. Their repertoire has evolved from marches exclusively to a wide variety of styles, from pop music to R&B and Christmas songs, arranged for the band's specific instrumentation of woodwinds, brasswinds, and percussion. The woodwinds include a large number of clarinets in various voices, saxophones, flutes, and oboe and bassoon; brasswinds include trumpets and trombones, alto horns, baritones and tubas; the percussion section uses *field drums* as well as glockenspiel and other types of pitched percussion instruments. Marching bands also can include stationary instrumentation, such as orchestral timpani and xylophones. These ensembles are often accompanied by so-called 'auxiliaries' such as dancers, color guards, and cheerleaders — as such, they're also called *show bands*. A *varsity band* is a college or university ('varsity') marching band.

Pep bands

A *pep band* is a subgroup of the marching band. It's a non-marching band that performs at sporting events (basketball, hockey, volleyball, etc.), to rouse team spirit. The repertoire may be comprised of anything from jazz and rock hits to Top 40 and traditional school songs. Pep bands come in any size, from a quartet to a thirty-piece band or an even larger group. The instrumentation includes mostly woodwinds, brasswinds, drums, percussion, and often electric guitar, bass guitar, and keyboards. They're also referred to as *stand bands*.

Jazz band

Many schools also have a jazz band, which is a stationary band much like a big band or jazz orchestra (see page 149).

More than one

Students often play in more than one group. The pep band may have a lot of the same faces that you'll see in the marching band or the jazz band, for example.

Orchestra

Most (beginning) school orchestras consist of string players only. Orchestras play more than classical music; their repertoire often includes popular music, television and movie themes, Broadway favorites, and so on. The *full orchestra* is made up of members of both the band (wind and percussion) and the orchestra.

Strolling strings

Strolling strings are an alternative to the traditional orchestra. The string players don't march, but stroll through the crowd at community events, banquets, art shows, and other functions, playing various types of popular music.

MORE BANDS

There are many types of uniformed marching and non-marching bands outside of the educational world. Some examples?

Drum corps

Drum and bugle corps, or *drum corps* for short, are often regarded as the sports of music. Though non-competitive corps do exist, drum corps are typically competitive efforts. Their competitions take place on football fields, with each highly stylized performance lasting some ten to twelve minutes. Traditionally, corps use brasswinds in the key of G only — commonly referred to as soprano bugles, alto bugles (such as mellophones), tenor bugles (baritone, euphonium), and bass bugles. Corps are now allowed to use brasswinds in alternative keys. In addition to field drums, these bands also use *pit percussion*, such as xylophones, marimbas, or timpani. Color guards, flags, rifles, or sabers, are an important element of the corps. Drum corps members can be of almost any age, from under seven to over sixty-five. Drums corps are regulated by organizations such as Drum Corps International (DCI), Drum Corps Associates (DCA), and DCUK.

Parade bands

There are different types of parade bands, which usually feature a combination of drums and other instruments such as bagpipes or fifes. *Ancient fife and drum corps* use keyed and keyless transverse flutes (fifes) and traditional rope-tensioned drums.

Scramble bands

Some 'marching' bands do not necessarily march; for example: *scramble bands*. Their instrumentation is a hodge-podge of everything from cellos and accordions to harps and bass guitar; even non-musicians can join in with pots and pans — literally.

Brass bands

Brass bands, which are comprised of brass and percussion, have British roots. The cornet is the brass band's leading voice. Most of the brass instruments used (e.g., flugelhorns, euphoniums, baritones, tubas) feature a conical bore (gradually becoming wider from the mouthpiece towards the bell), which makes for the warm, sweet, or mellow sound of the brass band. The repertoire may include marches, traditionals, folk songs, hymns, rags, and classical transcriptions, but also jazz and pop songs.

CLASSICAL MUSIC

Classical music is played by a variety of groups and ensembles dedicated strictly to the genre. The largest type of group is the *symphony orchestra*. (A symphony is a composition that typically consists of four large parts or movements.) Symphony orchestras usually have between fifty and more than a hundred members, with the majority of them playing strings. In large orchestras, there could be more than sixty string players (e.g., sixteen first violinists, fourteen second violinists, twelve violists, ten cellists and eight double bassists) in addition to sixteen woodwind players (flutes, clarinets, oboes, bassoons), sixteen brasswinds (trumpets, trombones, French horns, tuba), three to four percussionists, one or two timpanists, two harpists and a pianist. Other instruments may be included as well, such as a saxophone.

Philharmonic orchestra

A *Philharmonic orchestra* is just a different name for a symphony orchestra. The term 'philharmonic' can be translated as 'music-loving,' while the word 'symphony' basically means 'sounding together.'

Chamber orchestra

A *chamber orchestra* is similar, yet smaller. The number of string players typically varies from twenty to thirty, and there are two rather than four players for most wind instruments.

Ensemble

The term 'ensemble,' commonly implies a group featuring an instrumentalist for each musical part. In an orchestra, there is always more than one string player dedicated to each part.

Chamber ensembles

Chamber ensembles are typically subcategorized according to the primary featured instrument(s) and the number of players, such as the following examples:

- *String quartets*: two violins, one viola, one cello
- *String quintets*: two violins, two violas, one cello; or two violins, one viola, two cellos
- *Wind trios*: one clarinet, one bassoon, one French horn
- *Wind quintets*: one clarinet, one bassoon, one French horn, one oboe, one flute
- *Brass quintets*: two trumpets, one French horn, one trombone, one tuba or bass trombone
- *Piano trio*: one piano, one violin, one cello

Non-standard

An ensemble needn't be conventional or traditional to find musical works to play: There are many compositions available for nonstandard groups — trumpet and vocal, or three brasswinds and piano, and so on. Also, music written for one type of ensemble can be arranged for different instruments; for example, string quartet pieces have been arranged for four saxophonists. Tip: The term 'string quartet' can refer to both the ensemble and a work for that type of ensemble.

Contemporary music

There is no standard instrumentation common to ensembles that play *contemporary* classical music by twentieth and twenty-first century composers. These compositions may include arrangements for everything from electronic instruments to violins, anvils, horns, and radios.

THE SAME INSTRUMENT

A *clarinet choir* features most or all of the clarinet voices, from the small, high-pitched A♭ sopranino clarinet to the large, low-pitched bass clarinet. Similar ensembles exist for other instrumentalists, at all levels, from amateur to professional: There are *saxophone choirs*, *flute orchestras*, *accordion ensembles*, and so on. Some of these groups include a rhythm section (bass, drums), keyboards, or other instruments. The term 'orchestra' is usually reserved for the largest of these groups, often with fifty or more musicians. Repertoires can range from classical pieces to marches, international folk music, pop songs, and arrangements of compositions for concert bands and symphony orchestras.

VOCAL GROUPS

In a vocal group, all members 'play' the same instrument. Various labels are used for groups of singers. The term *choir* is often used for vocal groups in churches who sing sacred music or gospel songs, but there are secular groups that call themselves choirs as well. Other names are *chorus*, *chorale*, or *choral ensemble*. The smallest vocal groups also use the labels trio, quartet, and so on.

School choirs

Schools often have more than one choir. Some are open to all interested students, others require singing experience, an audition, or both.

Easy access

There are many vocal groups (boy, girl, or mixed) that your child can join without any previous experience, ranging from community choirs to church choirs. Their repertoires can vary from hymns to rock songs.

More

Joining a choir provides children with the opportunity to develop their voices, learn to sing and breathe correctly, work on their stage performance, etc. The amount of guidance provided to choir members regarding their vocal and musical development may differ per choir, of course: Some choirs sing just for fun; others have strong educational elements.

GUITARS, BASS, DRUMS AND MORE

With one or two guitars, a bass guitar, and a drum set, you can play the entire history of rock and roll and numerous more-or-less closely related styles — soul, gospel, country, R&B, funk…

Four elements

The typical rock band's instrumentation perfectly demonstrates the three major elements of this and many other types of music. The drummer provides the element of rhythm, in close cooperation with the bassist. The two together form band's foundation, or the basis, if you will. The vocalist (often one of the musicians, usually a guitarist) provides the element of melody of the song, aided by or trading this task with the solo guitarist. The second guitarist (the rhythm guitar player) plays chords, providing the element of harmony to the music.

More instruments

Many bands incorporate additional musicians, such as one or more keyboard players, a percussionist (coloring the music with congas, timbales, bells, cymbals, and so on), one or more horn players (trumpet, trombone, saxophone), or backing vocalists. The acoustic steel-string guitar is often used next to an electric guitar. Some bands use less

One of these guitars is used in rock bands; the other is a jazz guitar…

traditional instruments such as the (electric) violin, the flute, or a tuba. The turntable, played by a DJ, has found its place within quite a few bands as well (see page 172).

JAZZ

Jazz is a term that describes an enormous array of musical styles, and there jazz ensembles with all sorts of line-ups. The model for most jazz groups consists of a drummer and bassist (traditionally on double bass, but electric bass guitar is also used). For the harmonic element, the piano is used more often than the guitar. A 'standard' jazz quartet includes a drummer, bassist, and pianist, plus a (tenor or alto) saxophone or a trumpet; a jazz quintet typically has both types of saxophones.

Big band

A *big band*, a.k.a. *swing band*, *dance band* or *jazz orchestra* traditionally plays music from the 1930s and 1940s — the so-called 'swing era.' A typical big band has three to five trumpets and the same number of trombones, two alto and two tenor saxophones, and a baritone saxophone. Clarinet, flute, and other instruments may be included as well. The rhythm section is comprised of the drummer, the bassist, and a pianist, and possibly a guitarist, a percussionist, or a vibraphonist. Their repertoire often includes more contemporary compositions as well.

Dixieland

Some type of jazz bands have typical line-ups. In a Dixieland band, for example, you'll likely find a tuba rather than a string bass, a clarinet rather than a saxophone, a cornet rather than a trumpet, and a banjo rather than a guitar.

Today and tomorrow

In the jazz of today, any type of instrumentation is welcome. A trio of electric cello, piano, and tuba? No problem.

Fusion

Jazz has frequently been a favorite style for merging with other kinds of music; the possibilities for hybrid styles are endless. Fusion and jazz-rock bands often feature electric bass guitar, drums, keyboards (piano or electronic keyboard instruments), electric guitar, and one or more horns, for example.

Instruments

Electric guitars come in many different guises. Page 148 shows two extremes. Likewise, a jazz drum set is quite different from the kit a symphonic-rock drummer may use; the latter will typically incorporate more and larger drums and cymbals.

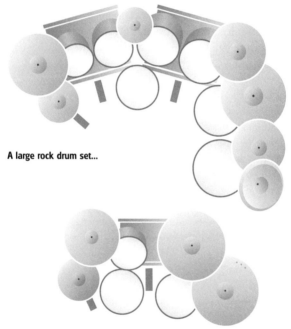

A large rock drum set...

... and a four-piece jazz set.

AND MORE

There are many more types of bands, which are often correlated to specific styles, and some use very specific instruments. Again, some random examples:

- In a *bluegrass band*, you'll find guitars, a double bass, a fiddle (a violin that's played and possibly tuned differently), a five-string banjo, and a mandolin.
- A *klezmer band* plays Jewish folk music. The violin and clarinet are important voices that are often accompanied

A five-string banjo, used in bluegrass and other styles of music.

by another violin (playing rhythmic patterns, just like in traditional gypsy music), as well as an accordion, drums (bass drum, snare drum, cymbals), and a brasswind bass instrument.

· A typical *salsa band*, playing what could be described as New York Latin music, has no less than three percussionists (playing bongos, congas, and timbales), a bassists, one or more singers, and horns (trumpet, trombone, saxophones and/ or flute).

timbales with cowbells

congas

A salsa band uses timbales, cowbells,
and congas, as well as bongos and other small percussion instruments.

· The Mexican *mariachi* combines standard instruments such as the violin, trumpet, and acoustic guitar with typical Mexican instruments such as the *vihuela* (a small, round-backed five-string guitar), a Mexican harp, and the *guitarron* (a large guitar-like instrument that plays the bass part).

• And then there are more than enough small and large groups playing *non-Western music* to fill another series of Tipbooks. Most non-Western cultures have their own musical styles and instruments.

9. THE INSTRUMENTS

Though you're probably familiar with many of the instruments mentioned in this book, the information in the following chapter may give you a better understanding of the differences between families of instruments, as well as of the instruments themselves. Most importantly, this chapter focuses on instruments accessible to beginning players. For more detailed information, please refer to the Tipbook on a particular instrument, or other instrument-specific resources.

Classifying instruments is just as difficult as classifying bands and orchestras. For example, the violin and the double bass are orchestral string instruments, but they're also frequently used outside of orchestras. They're also considered *bowed instruments* because they're played with a bow, although the strings of the double bass are often plucked instead. The bass guitar belongs to the family of fretted string instruments, but many bassists play fretless versions. The piano is technically a percussion instrument (because the hammers hit the piano strings much like a drummer hits drum heads), but it also qualifies as a string instrument (it has more strings than any other instrument!); and this book classifies it as a keyboard instrument.

STRING INSTRUMENTS
The family of string or stringed instruments has two main subgroups: the *orchestral strings*, or simply 'strings,' and the *fretted string instruments* such as the guitar. Unlike orchestral string instruments, guitars and bass guitars

have small metal bars (*frets*) on the fingerboard. Frets make playing in tune easier: It is the exact position of the fret that produces the exact pitch of the note you play, rather than the exact position of your finger. So why don't violins have frets? Because they'd make the instrument sound quite different.

Violin.

Double bass.

Orchestral string instruments Tipcodes KIDS-005, KIDS-006, KIDS-007

The violin is the most widely played orchestral string instrument. It's used for numerous musical styles, from classical to gypsy jazz to country. The viola is slightly larger and, consequently, sounds slightly lower. Its highest three strings sound the same pitch as the lowest three violin strings (G, D, A), and its fourth string sounds a lower C. The cello is considerably larger yet. Its four strings are tuned to the same notes as viola strings, only an octave lower (C, G, D, A). The cello and the viola are not often found outside of classical circles, but there's no reason why they shouldn't be — some musicians even use these instruments for heavy metal songs!

Double bass   Tipcode KIDS-008

The double bass (a.k.a. *upright bass*, *string bass*) looks like the big brother of the other three, but it's actually more of a distant cousin. It typically features sloped shoulders and a flat back, rather than an arched one. The tuning is different as well — the strings are a fourth apart rather than a fifth, and tuned to E, A, D, G, from low to high. Another difference is that a double bass has metal tuning machines, rather than the wooden tuning pegs of a violin or cello. This instrument is frequently used outside of the classical realm (mainly in jazz), in which case it is usually plucked instead of bowed.

Guitars

The guitar comes in many sizes and shapes. First, let's start with acoustic and electric guitars.

Acoustic guitars   Tipcode KIDS-009

There are two basic types of acoustic guitars: those with nylon strings, and those with steel strings. They look similar at first sight, but their bodies feature different shapes and sizes, their heads (at the very end of the neck) are different, and steel-string guitars have a narrower neck. Nylon-string guitars or *Spanish guitars* are mostly used for classical music. The *steel-string guitar* has a brighter, slightly louder sound that lends itself better to pop, country, or folk music. Steel-string guitars are available in various models, from the large Jumbo and Dreadnought guitars to the small Concert guitar.

Classical, Spanish, or nylon-string guitar.

Steel-string, western, or folk guitar.

Electric guitars

The most popular electric guitar designs haven't changed much since their introduction in the early 1950s. Most electric guitars have a solid body rather than a hollow,

Gibson Les Paul®

Fender Stratocaster®

"... hardly changed since the 1950s..."

resonating sound box. That's why they hardly produce any sound without an amplifier (which makes them great for silent practice!). One, two, or even more pickups literally pick up the vibrations of the strings and convert them to electrical signals. These signals are sent to an amplifier, which boosts them and sends them to a speaker. Jazz players typically use a particular type of electric guitar that features a hollow body with an arched top, and two *f-holes*, just like a violin (see page 148).

Acoustic-electrics, semi-solids, double-necks Tipcode KIDS-010

There are many variations on the guitar: *acoustic-electrics* (acoustic guitars with a built-in pickup), *double-neck* guitars (one six-string neck and one twelve-string neck, or one guitar neck and one bass guitar neck), *semi-solid* electrics, *resonator* guitars (guitars with a metal body and built-in resonators), *flamenco* guitars, and so on. And if that isn't enough, most 'electric' guitars are used with one or more effects to color and add to their sound.

Bass guitar   Tipcode KIDS-011

The bass guitar, also introduced in the early 1950s, has the same type of body and neck as an electric guitar and the same tuning as a double bass. Next to the traditional four-string model, there are bass guitars with five, six, and even more strings. Fretless bass guitars have become quite common (yet not for beginning players).

Electric violins

Guitars and basses are not the only stringed instruments that come in electric versions. There are *electric violins* (with or without frets, and with four or more strings), and a few companies make *electric cellos* and *upright basses*. Some

A seven-string electric violin with frets (Wood Violins).

electric violins and cellos are specifically designed for silent practice, as shown on page 78.

Harp
The harp is played by plucking the strings, typically with eight fingers. A harp has more strings than a guitar but fewer than a piano. To be able to play music in various keys, you need to adjust the pitch of a number of those strings. On a *lever harp* you do this by adjusting a number of levers. The *pedal harp*, a very expensive instrument, has a set of pedals that allow you to adjust the pitch of various strings in one move. Harpists will find that the greatest selection of harp music is from the classical genre, but there are also folk and pop compositions for harp.

Mandolin.

Mandolin
The original *mandolin* is clearly related to the lute; today's mandolins, however, look quite different. They still have a short neck, but they feature an arched top (though flat-top models are available too) and often a flat back. A mandolin has four pairs of strings.

Banjo
The *banjo* (see page 151) has a round body with a plastic 'skin' for a top, just like a drum. It has four or five strings and a very short, percussive sound, and is usually played with finger picks. Five-string banjos, like the mandolin, are mainly used in bluegrass and country. The four-string version is often played in folk and Dixieland bands.

Saz, bouzouki, balalaika...
Most cultures have their own string instruments. One example is the Turkish *saz-baglama*, more commonly

known as the *saz*, with adjustable frets, a long neck, and a relatively small body. Others include the somewhat similar-looking Greek *bouzouki*; the long-necked Russian *balalaika*, with its triangular body; the Bulgarian *tambura*, with a very shallow, pear-shaped body and four pairs of strings. The list is virtually endless.

A balalaika, from Russia.

WOODWINDS

The recorder is one of the most basic woodwind instruments. All its family members work along the same principle. If you play the instrument, you make the air column inside the instrument's body vibrate — and vibrating air is sound. You can play various notes by closing and opening one or more of the toneholes in the woodwind's body (by doing so, you vary the effective length of the body, and thus the length of the air column, changing the tone). When all toneholes are closed, the air column is at its maximum length, and the recorder will produce its lowest note. With each tonehole you open, from the lowest one up, the air column gets shorter and a higher note will sound.

Non-wood woodwinds

As you will see below, woodwind instruments aren't necessarily made of wood: Saxophones are made of brass; most flutes have a metal body (wooden flutes are very expensive); and many student clarinets, oboes, and piccolos have a plastic body.

Plastic

Plastic oboes and clarinets are more durable than their

wooden counterparts; they also need less care and maintenance, and they're weather resistant. The wooden
models usually produce a warmer, darker tone. This is
not because they're made of wood, but because they're
typically better-constructed, higher-quality instruments
than the plastic student models.

Flute   Tipcodes KIDS-012, KIDS-013

The flute is a *transverse* or *side-blown* instrument with a
number of keys that cover the toneholes. Original flutes were
made of wood; nowadays, most flute players opt for a
metal version. Just about all student flutes are silver-plated.
The more money you spend on an instrument, the more
parts will be made of solid silver. Solid silver parts enhance
both the instrument's sound and its longevity. The piccolo
is a higher-pitched flute with either a plastic (student
models), metal, or wooden body. There are also lower-
pitched flutes such as the *alto flute* and the rare *bass flute*.

Clarinet   Tipcode KIDS-014

The clarinet has the same type of keys as a flute. The body
is usually made of plastic (for student instruments) or wood,
but there are metal clarinets as well. A major difference
between the flute and the clarinet is in the way the sound
is generated: The clarinet has a mouthpiece with a single
piece of *cane* — the reed — attached to it. When you play
the instrument, the reed vibrates, which makes the air
inside the instrument vibrate. The main clarinet voice is
the B♭ clarinet. Other popular voices are the higher-
pitched E♭ clarinet, and the lower sounding A, *alto*, and
bass clarinets.

Saxophone   Tipcodes KIDS-015, KIDS-016, KIDS-017, KIDS-018

Likewise, the saxophone has a similar key mechanism, and
its mouthpiece is very similar to that of the clarinet:
They're both *single-reed instruments*. The major difference
is that the clarinet has a largely cylindrical body, while the
saxophone has a conical body: It gets steadily wider from
the mouthpiece onwards. This makes it sound and play
quite differently. Alto and tenor saxophones are the most
widely used voices, followed by the larger *baritone saxophone* and the smaller *soprano sax*. Saxophones are made
of brass, but they still belong to the woodwind family.

Oboe and bassoon

Tipcode KIDS-019

The oboe and the bassoon are also reed instruments, but they each feature a *double reed* — two pieces of cane tied together on one end. The oboe has a conical body, like the saxophone. Student models are made of plastic, while professional models are made of wood. The bassoon is a large and expensive instrument with a body that consists of two wooden (or plastic) 'tubes.' The reed is attached to the *bocal*, a curved metal tube. Players usually support the instrument with a seat strap, a neck strap, or a special type of support. The *contrabassoon* is a lower-pitched version of the bassoon. The *English horn*, another double-reed instrument, is the only woodwind that's officially known as a 'horn'.

BRASSWINDS

Brasswinds do not have a vibrating reed; instead, they're played by vibrating (or 'buzzing') your lips in the instrument's mouthpiece. Larger brasswinds have larger mouthpieces. The buzzing lips are sometimes referred to as the lip reed, and some call brasswinds lip-reed instruments.

A trumpet mouthpiece.

Different pitches

On brasswinds, you play notes of different pitches using your 'embouchure' (simply put: the way you blow the instrument) and by varying the total length of the instrument with a number of valves, or with a slide. If you extend the slide of a trombone, you're making the instrument longer,

Pressing the first valve adds the length of the U-shaped piece of tubing at the first piston.

which allows for lower-pitched notes. A trombone slide has seven positions. Likewise, the three valves of a trumpet allow for a total of seven positions, making for seven different total tube lengths. (Pressing a valve forces the air in the instrument to make a small detour, making for a longer air column).

Conical instruments   Tipcode KIDS-020

Trumpets are a bit harder to blow and they sound brighter than most other brasswinds. This is because the tube (the 'body') of a trumpet is much less conical than that of other brasswinds, offering more resistance. If you compare a trumpet to a flugelhorn, for example, you will see that the latter flares much more, making it easier to blow while producing a much warmer, mellower sound.

The flugelhorn (below) looks quite different from the trumpet. Cornets fall in between these two instruments.

Cornet

There are two basic types of cornet: the British or European model, and the American cornet. The latter looks much longer, but the length of their tubing is identical. The *American cornet* is more like the trumpet, whereas the *British cornet* or *short cornet* is more like the flugelhorn.

French horn

Its circular tubing gives the French horn a very different look from other brasswinds. It has a very different timbre as well, and its mouthpiece is small compared to other brasswinds. Another difference is the contribution by the player's right hand: The player moves it within the bell of the instrument to control the timbre and the exact pitch of the notes.

Low brass, background brass

Most brass instruments listed above are sometimes categorized as *soprano* or *treble* (high-pitched) *brasswinds*. Lower-pitched brasswinds are known as *low brass*, which usually includes the tenor and bass trombone as well. Many low brass instruments also belong to the category of background brasswinds: They're typically used 'in the background' as an accompaniment for other (brass) instruments. Still, the tuba and all other background instruments can be used for soloing as well.

Tuba

The word 'tuba' commonly refers to the bass tuba, which has a tube around twenty-five feet (!) long. Bass tubas come in C, for symphony orchestras, and in B♭, for brass bands,

A bass tuba.

concert bands, and other wind ensembles. Tubas pitched in F and E♭ are one size smaller. The low pitches of the tuba are typically indicated as CC ('double C'), BB♭ ('double B-flat'), FF, and EE♭.

Euphonium

The tenor tuba, pitched one octave higher than the bass tuba, is often referred to as a 'euphonium.'

Saxhorns

Around 1845, when Adolph Sax was still perfecting his saxophone, he was granted a patent on a whole family of *saxhorns*, from large to small. Some of those instruments are still in use, such as the tenor horn and the baritone. The baritone is very similar to the euphonium, but a euphonium has a wider bore and a larger bell. As a result, it sounds somewhat bigger and warmer. The two lowest-sounding saxhorns are pretty much the same instruments as the large B♭ and E♭ tubas.

Confusing

Many brass instruments have different names in different countries. For example, a euphonium is called *tenor tuba* in some countries, and *bass tuba* or *alto horn* in others.

Marching brasswinds

Regular tubas, horns, and trombones are tricky to play while marching. The industry has come up with various alternatives for making things easier. A well-known example is the *sousaphone*: a 'circular tuba' with an enormous, forward-facing bell, which is often made of a lighter, synthetic material to save weight.

On your shoulder

You can also get trumpet-shaped euphoniums, tubas, and other brass instruments designed so you can rest them on your left shoulder, making them easier to march with. The bells of these instruments point forwards instead of upwards, so the sound is projected toward the audience. Some companies make *convertible instruments*: You switch from an upright tuba to a marching instrument by removing the valve section, turning the instrument around, and reinstalling the valve section.

A sousaphone.

Without valves

Brass instruments without valves are referred to as *natural instruments*. Some examples are the natural trumpet or clarion, the hunting horn, and the bugle.

KEYBOARD INSTRUMENTS

The one thing all keyboard instruments have in common is the keyboard. Although this feature is the same for all keyboard instruments, playing the piano is quite different from playing an organ, for example. One major difference is that where a piano note decays after a moment, an organ will sound until you let go of the key.

Piano   Tipcode KIDS-021

The piano is often considered the world's most versatile acoustic instrument. It sounds notes lower than a bass and higher than a piccolo; you can plan chords, bass lines, and melodies on it — all at the same time. It can be used in almost any style of music, all by itself, to accompany a choir, or as a solo instrument with a large orchestra, and so on. It's also the favorite instrument of many composers, and a great secondary instrument for any musician — if only because the layout of the keyboard makes many musical concepts easier to understand.

Digital piano

A *digital piano* doesn't have strings. Instead, it uses *samples*: digital recordings of piano (and other) sounds. The specific feel of a piano keyboard, caused by the complicated mechanism that makes the hammers hit the strings, is mimicked on higher-quality digital pianos. Even though today's digital piano sounds and feels really close to the acoustic instrument, many (mainly classical) pianists still find it a different instrument. This has much to do with the fact that the sound is produced by speakers rather than by a large wooden soundboard. The main advantages of digital pianos are that they cost less and require less maintenance, they weigh much less, they can be played with headphones, they usually come equipped with a built-in sequencer to record what you play, and many other features (various sounds, effects, and so on). On the other hand, acoustic pianos last much longer, have a higher resale value — and they have the true sound and feel of an acoustic piano.

Hybrid piano

A *hybrid piano* offers the best of both worlds. It's an acoustic piano equipped with a built-in digital piano. If silent practice is required, a pedal- or lever-operated rail stops the hammers from hitting the strings as a sound module provides the sampled piano sounds, or any other sounds available, from strings to vibraphone.

Home keyboard

A *home keyboard* is an easily accessible instrument featuring numerous built-in sounds (samples, again), ranging from saxophones and flutes, to electric guitars, passing trains, synthesized sounds, percussion, and strings. Piano sounds are also included, but most home keyboards don't sound as natural as digital pianos, and they don't have a piano-type (*hammer action*) keyboard. One of the main features of a home keyboard is the accompaniment section. This built-in virtual ensemble supplements your playing with chords, bass lines, drums and percussion, strings, and so on: Home keyboards are true one-man orchestras.

Organ

Today's electronic *organs* and home keyboards are very similarly equipped, with a few exceptions: Organs have more organ sounds, they always come with bass pedals, and they have a volume pedal and twin keyboards. There are non-electronic organs as well.

Synthesizer

While a home keyboard basically has preset sounds and an accompaniment section, a *synthesizer* allows you to create (*synthesize*) completely original sounds. These instruments provide you with raw samples or electronically generated tones and a wide range of electronic filters, allowing you to mold sounds into almost any shape you like. The difference between home keyboards, synths, and other electronic keyboard instruments (e.g., *samplers*, *workstations*, *groove machines*) isn't always really clear, as there is a growing number of common features. Synthesizers are not typically chosen by beginning musicians.

Accordion

The *accordion* is another keyboard instrument. You might see it as a wind instrument too: Its tone is produced in a way similar to that of a *harmonica* or *mouth harp*. The left hand plays the chords, operating a button keyboard where each single button triggers a chord. The right hand plays the melody, operating either a button keyboard (a.k.a. chromatic keyboard) or a keyboard with a standard piano-type layout.

DRUMS AND PERCUSSION

The family of drums and percussion instruments is probably the largest family of musical instruments, comprising basically everything that produces a sound when hit or shaken. Drum set players usually play drum kit only, and the timpani in a symphony orchestra are played by a dedicated timpanist. Many other drummers and percussionists play a whole range of instruments. For percussion students, this includes the snare drum, one or more of the mallet instruments, tympani, and other instruments. Percussionists in (pop, fusion, Latin, etc.) bands usually play a large variety of instruments, from congas, bongos and timbales, to bells, shakers, and an infinite collection of related gear.

Drums

There are three types of drums found in marching bands, concert bands, and symphony orchestras — snare, bass, and toms — and it's these same three drums that form the basis of a drum set. In each type of band, these drums may have different dimensions and tunings, but their main characteristics are the same:

- The *snare drum* produces a tight, crisp, articulate sound. Its drum heads are tuned very tightly. The crisp sound is produced by a set of (wire) snares under the lower head.
- The *bass drum* sounds like its name suggests.
- A series of *toms* in different sizes, with lower and higher tunings, provide the melodic element in the drum section.

Field drums

Marching drummers typically use deep-shelled snare drums, relatively shallow bass drums, and single-headed toms known as *tenor drums*, *multi-tenors*, or *timp toms*. The specific types of drums used by marching drummers are known as *field drums*, and they're sometimes referred to as *marching drums*.

Orchestral drums

Orchestral drummers use a shallower type of snare drum. Their bass drum is usually much bigger (it doesn't need to be carried around!). The single-headed toms are called *concert toms*.

Drum set   Tipcode KIDS-022

In a *drum set*, all featured drums are played by a single drummer. The snare drum stands between the drummer's legs and the bass drum is played with a pedal-operated beater. In a standard five-piece setup, two small, double-headed toms are mounted on the bass drum (*mounted toms* or *rack toms*). A third tom, the *floor tom*, has its own three legs.

A standard five-piece drum set (five drums, two cymbals, a pair of hi-hats, and two pedals).

Cymbals

A set drummer also uses a number of *cymbals* in different sizes and thicknesses. Among them is a pair of cymbals that are played with another pedal, the *hi-hat pedal*. Marching and orchestral drummers play cymbal pairs, striking one against the other.

Timpani

Timpani are a very different type of drum. They produce a clearly identifiable pitch (they're tuned to specific notes, unlike snare drums, bass drums, and toms), and they have a kettle instead of a cylindrical shell. Timpani are used in orchestras and pit percussion sections.

Melodic percussion

Melodic percussion instruments have metal or wooden keys arranged in a way similar to piano keyboards. The fact that they're played with mallets explains their other name, *mallet instruments*.

- A *glockenspiel* has a series of small metal keys, producing a piercing, bell-like sound. Orchestral glockenspiels are also known as *orchestral bells*.
- *Xylophones*, used in both marching and orchestral settings, have narrow wooden or plastic keys with small resonators.
- A *marimba* has wider, larger wooden keys with large resonators, making for a much warmer tone.
- The *vibraphone* is mainly used in jazz bands. Its wide metal keys have resonators with rotating metal discs that make the instrument's sound 'vibrate'.

Latin percussion

The best-known Latin percussion instruments include congas, bongos, timbales, and cowbells (see page 151). These instruments are the driving force in a salsa band, but they're also used in jazz bands, rock bands, and related types of groups. Latin percussionists also use an almost endless range of other instruments to spice up the music, as mentioned before. Many of these instruments are also available in kid's versions.

More percussion instruments

There are many more percussion instruments. Each

culture seems to have its own assortment. Some of these instruments are easily accessible for beginning players, such as the African *djembe*, which is often used in drum circles. The traditional wooden djembe is frequently replaced by Western variations with a modern tuning system rather than ropes, a fiberglass shell and a plastic head. It slightly resembles the Turkish *darbuka*, a vase drum with a metal shell. Brazilian drums, such as the large *surdo* and the high-pitched *repinique*, are used outside of samba bands as well. Many other types of drums are rarely used by beginners, such as the Latin-American *cajon* (the player sits on this multi-toned wooden box while playing it), the Indian *tabla* (two small drums that produce a multitude of pitches and tones), and Japanese drums, like the giant *odaiko*, a drum that may weigh close to five hundred pounds.

COMPUTERS AND TURNTABLES

If took some time before computers and turntables were considered musical instruments, but they can definitely be used as such.

The computer

Thousands of songs these days are composed, arranged — and played, and recorded — with nothing but a digital keyboard instrument hooked up to a computer. Many kids and teens love to express themselves musically this way. The computer houses sampled sounds (see page 166) of every instrument you can think of, and the player triggers these sounds from a piano-type digital keyboard hooked up to the computer. These sounds can be recorded layer by layer using the computer's sequencing software: first the bass, then the drums, a piano part, strings, horns, a guitar solo; the possibilities are endless. The music can also be arranged and edited on the computer (assigning other voices to parts; changing the key of the song, altering the timing or the pitch of single notes, and so on). Ready? Then the same computer can be used to burn the music onto a CD, and even to print the scores of all the individual parts of the composition. You can also use the computer to record acoustic instruments, of course. Or you can make a score as you would on paper, then assign voices to the notes and have the computer play the music, and so on. The possibilities are truly infinite. The required software (a sequencing program that 'records' the music, and a score editor) ranges from freeware to expensive professional tools.

Turntables

Originally, the turntable was nothing more than a record player, but it has turned into a valid musical instrument. DJs (or *turntablists*) entertain the crowd by carefully choosing and mixing a sequence of songs (changing their tempo, creating new rhythms by playing two songs simultaneously, and so on). Some DJs join a band where they manipulate the records by hand while operating one or more faders to produce percussive sounds, riffs, and special effects (from echoes and flare scratches to loopings and hydroplanes…). Records, commonly referred to as 'vinyl,' are also used to add rhythm or harmonies to the music.

10. BEING PREPARED

A dry throat, butterflies in your stomach, jitters and shakes, weak knees, trembling fingers, a throbbing heart... all familiar sensations experienced by most anyone who ever stood on a stage to perform, audition, or took a music exam (and those who claim they never experience such symptoms are often said to be lying or dead!).

Nervousness and performing go hand in hand. It's a sign that you're undergoing an adrenaline rush, and without it, performances may be less exciting for both the players and the audience. But the anxiousness can get so bad that it causes you to fail an audition, not make the grade, or mess up the performance. This chapter shares some ideas on reducing audition anxiety, stage fright, and exam nerves.

Books
Many books have been written on this subject, and there is a whole lot more be said and taught about it. The following tips touch the mere basics; and as obvious as they seem, they're often quite effective.

Adults and kids
Kids seem to suffer less from jitters and other anxiety symptoms than most teens and adults. So one of the best ways to prevent such feelings in the first place is to begin performing in public at an early age, be it with a school band, playing mini-recitals for you or the family every week or after each practice session — even if it's only briefly. As taking this advice may not be an option if you're already beyond early childhood, keep reading...

PREPARING YOURSELF

First, a look at what could, or should, be done beforehand.

Practice, practice, practice

Children — and adults — who are not fully prepared for a performance, an audition, or an exam have every reason to be nervous. Practicing efficiently under the guidance of a teacher who should of course be aware of your child's upcoming performance, is one key to abating anxiety. A tip: The closer the time of the main event comes, the more important it is to focus practice sessions on problem areas, rather than on playing known material. A rule of thumb is to be able to play the tricky bits at least five to ten times in a row without stumbling; only then can you be sure that you've got them down. Tip: Make yourself start over from the beginning after each mistake, even if it's the very last note. This can make playing the final run almost as thrilling as an audition.

Too late

If you feel that you have to spend hours practicing the day before the performance, or on the actual day, you probably failed to use your previous practice sessions to the fullest. For horn players, practicing too long or too briefly in advance may cause them to have lip trouble during the performance.

Slips

Even professionals make mistakes, so preparing a piece includes preparing for stumbles and slips. Practice how to recover quickly and continue to play in the correct tempo. Teachers have tips on how to deal with slip-ups, such as not making a face, which will just draw everyone's attention to your mistake. Some teachers even specialize in audition preparation.

Memory

You may play from memory to impress the jury, but con-sider bringing your sheet music along if memorization was not required. Having it there will make it easier to start over if you do slip. Does your piece require page turning? Then it would be helpful to memorize the first section on the following page. Another tip: Make sure you make a list of the pieces you're going to play and bring it with you; it doesn't look good if you've forgotten the title of your next piece.

Accompanist

If you're going to play with an accompanist during the performance, it's best if that's the person you rehearse with as well. Playing with a stranger can cause added tension, and a familiar face can be a great confidence booster. Even if not required, you may want to consider doing your piece with accompaniment (if you're not already the pianist or guitarist): Having another person there may help reduce stress, and it usually makes for a more entertaining performance too.

Deal with it

No matter how well-prepared you are, exams, auditions, and performances will induce stress and nervousness. Dealing with this is part of the learning process of playing, period. Practice doesn't make perfect, but the more you play (and the more exams or auditions you do), the better you will eventually become at handling stage fright.

Surrender

Fighting your nerves is not a good idea either: Doing so can even add to your stress level, which is probably already substantial. Telling yourself to be calm usually doesn't work either. You aren't calm, so it's actually better to just surrender to that. The fact that your nerves can make your performance less than brilliant just shows how important it is to be well-prepared.

Mock auditions

The more used to playing for an audience you are, the less likely you are to be nervous for auditions or exams. Still, these situations are different from regular performances: They occur less frequently and there's usually a lot riding on them. A mistake made during a performance typically has fewer consequences than a slip at an audition. Staging *mock auditions* (a.k.a. *placebo auditions* or *dress rehearsals*) often helps in getting used to the extra tension. They can take place at home, while playing for family and friends; and some teachers organize mock auditions too. Tip: Turn mock auditions into a complete performance, including a formal entrance into the room, presenting yourself, and so on. Also, ask your audience to evaluate your playing afterwards to ensure that they were attentive to every note you played. Scary? That's the idea.

Recording in advance

Recording the pieces you'll be playing at the audition or exam can by very effective. First, a recording allows you to listen and evaluate your performance, as it's very difficult to do that while you're playing. And the recorded results can give you the objectivity you need to really assess what you're doing. Second, a simple recording device can have the same effect as an attentive audience in that it can make you nervous enough to perhaps make the kind of mistakes you would in front of a real audience. Getting used to the presence of a recording device is quite similar to getting used to an audience, so that makes it effective training. Don't forget to evaluate the recording, and don't listen for mistakes only. Pay close attention to timing, intonation, dynamics, and all other elements that make for a great performance, including tone. Evaluating the latter requires good recording and playback equipment. Tip: First warm up, and then try to play your prepared pieces and scales right during the first take — just like in real life!

Presentation

Are you required or do you want to dress a certain way for the performance? Then decide beforehand what you're going to wear, how to wear your hair, etc. Don't wait until the day of the show to do this, but get your look together at least the day before.

Sleep

And don't forget: A good night's sleep, or a nap before an afternoon performance, often works wonders!

SHOW TIME

There are many remedies for reducing nerves on the day of your performance too. First of all, leave home early so there's no need to rush, and make sure there's plenty of time to prepare for the performance once you're on site.

Relax

For some, simply repeating the words, 'I'm calm, I'm cool,' is enough to help them relax, but most people need more than this. There are many different techniques, ranging from deep-breathing exercises to meditation, yoga, or special methods like the Alexander Technique. You may also benefit from simple stretching, jumping, and other physical movement, and for some, screaming helps.

Transfer your stress

Another idea is to find a physical release for your stress. For example, take a paperclip along and hold it when you feel nervous, imagining that all of your extra energy is being drawn through your hand into the paperclip — then throw it away before you go onstage.

Warming-up

Warm-up routines (long notes, scales, and so on) not only get you musically prepared to perform, they can also help you relax. Long, slow notes are more effective than up-tempo riffs, obviously. If you feel the need to go through your scales and prepared pieces once more, you probably aren't really ready. Tip: Find a quiet place to prepare, if possible.

Silence

If there's no opportunity to actually play before you go onstage, just moving your fingers over the keys or the strings of your instrument will help. Wind instrument players can warm up their instrument by blowing warm air through it.

The instrument

Make sure the instrument is in good repair, and thoroughly check it before the performance. Exam judges may forgive a broken string, a failed reed, or a stuck valve, but even so, these things won't promote a confident performance. Brasswind players: If you've warmed up to prepare for your performance, make sure to drain your horn before going onstage.

Tuning and warming-up

Tuning the instrument under the observant eyes of your audience, the jurors, or the examiners may be nerve-wracking, so make sure you take care of this in advance, if possible.

Try it out

Pianists will usually play auditions or take exams on an unfamiliar instrument. Find out if it's possible to try out the instrument you'll be using in advance in order to get used to its feel and sound. The same goes for other musicians who must use house instruments.

Imagine

Many musicians fight their nerves by conjuring calming imagery. They imagine playing at home or on their favorite stage rather than in front of a jury; or they concentrate on a recent holiday, or pretend they're on a deserted island. Others promise themselves that this is their very last performance ever, so they need to give it all — now or never.

Pep talk

Giving yourself a pep talk may help too. But rather than just telling yourself to be cool and calm, tell yourself that you wouldn't even be here if your teacher hadn't thought you were ready — you've earned your way there.

Focus

Don't focus on the outcome of the audition or exam. Instead, concentrate on your music, as that's really what it's all about. What may also help is to make your objective the demonstration of your piece's beauty, rather than how impressive a player you are. Final tip before going in: Smile when you enter the room. This makes you both look and feel better.

A different type of audience

Auditioners and examiners are a particular kind of audience: They're there to judge your playing, rather than just enjoy the music. Still, it's good to realize that they're there for you; know that they want you to play your best and to make you feel at ease.

Any audience

It may help to calm you if you look at your examiners and auditioners the same way you'd look at a 'regular' audience:

Tell yourself that they're all very kind people (which they usually are, so this shouldn't be too hard.) Make eye contact with your jurors just as you would any other audience, and smile. And just as you might focus on the people you know, or the ones responding favorably to you in a regular performance, focus on the juror who smiles back at you.

Imagine
Another approach is to completely ignore the audience (imagine that you're playing at home alone); but realize that this might not work at an audition or an exam. A popular method is to image the audience (large or small, jurors or not) sitting in their underwear, feeling even more uncomfortable than you are onstage. Or think of the audience as non-musicians who will be impressed by every single note you play, or as the ultimate experts who showed up just to hear you…

The first note
Take a couple of seconds before you start playing. Breathe. Get the tempo of the piece going in your head, or even sing the first few bars in your mind; imagine yourself playing the song. Then it's time for the first note. Make it sound great, and enjoy your performance!

AND MORE
If none of the above works for you or your child, try consulting one of the many books on the subject. Another option is to take a yoga or meditation course, for example, or consider a drama class. Your child's music teacher may have additional tips, and do suggest that your child to talk to friends to learn how they deal with the problem.

Food and drinks
Various types of food and drink are said make anxiety worse (e.g., coffee, tea, and other products with caffeine, sugar, or salt), while others help to soothe your nerves. Bananas contain potassium, which helps you relax, and there are various types of calming herbal teas, for example. Alcohol may make you feel more relaxed, but it definitely inhibits motor skills, judgment, and clarity — so avoid drinking alcoholic beverages.

Drugs

Many professional musicians take *beta blockers* (heart medication, actually) to combat their performance anxiety. This type of drug is considered relatively safe, and it works a lot faster than a yoga course and most other relaxation techniques. But you should wonder if music is your thing if you need drugs to do it, even if it's only for high-stress situations, like an audition. Try instead to reduce if not eliminate stressors; only do things that make you feel good, and avoid those that induce anxiety. Music is supposed to be fun!

GLOSSARY

This glossary contains brief definitions and descriptions of some of the lesser known terms used in this book. Most other terms are explained as they are introduced: Please consult the index on pages 196–199.

Band instruments Instruments that are used in marching bands, concert bands, and so on. They're mainly woodwinds, brasswinds, and percussion instruments.

Bowed instruments See: *String instruments, stringed instruments.*

Brasswinds Trumpets, trombones, baritones, euphoniums, and similar instruments are referred to as brasswinds or brasswind instruments. Brasswinds are also known as *lip-reed instruments*. Not all brass instruments are brasswinds: The saxophone, though made of brass, is a woodwind.

Ear training Learning to recognize notes, intervals, scales, chords, etc. by ear, which is extremely helpful in understanding and reproducing music.

Fractional sizes Versions of violins and other string instruments (violas, cellos,

double basses, guitars) in reduced sizes. For example, a $^1/_{16}$ violin is about half as big as the $^4/_4$, full-size instrument.

Fretted instruments See: *String instruments, stringed instruments.*

Horn A term many woodwind and brasswind players refer their instrument by — whether a French horn, trumpet, or saxophone.

Instrumentation The combination of instruments in a musical group.

Keyboard instruments All instruments with a keyboard, such as piano, organ, and home keyboard.

Orchestral instruments Instruments used in orchestras, such as violins, violas, cellos, and woodwind instruments.

Orchestral strings The string instruments of (symphony, chamber, etc.) orchestras: the violin, the viola, the cello, and the double bass.

Percussion instruments A large group of instruments typically struck or hit (with bare hands, sticks, mallets, or other types of beaters) to sound. This family also includes instruments played by shaking (maracas, shekeres) or rubbing (guiro), for example.

Plucked instruments See: *String instruments, stringed instruments.*

Reed instruments Wind instruments played when a single or a double reed vibrates via your air stream. Clarinets and saxophones are single-reed instruments; the bassoon and the oboe are double-reed instruments.

Single-reed instruments See: *Reed instruments.*

Double-reed instruments See: *Reed instruments.*

String instruments, stringed instruments Terms often used to indicate orchestral string instruments (violin, viola, cello,

double bass) only. These are also known as *bowed instruments* or *strings*. Another group of stringed instruments are referred to as *fretted instruments*, such as guitars, mandolins, and banjos, or *plucked instruments* (which then includes the harp as well).

Fretted instruments See: *String instruments, stringed instruments.*

Strings 1. The strings on a stringed instrument or a piano. 2. The orchestral string instruments. See: *String instruments, stringed instruments.*

Wind instruments Instruments that sound when blown, such as trumpets, clarinets, and flutes. Two main subgroups are woodwinds and brasswinds. See: *Woodwinds, Brasswinds.*

Woodwinds Flutes and reed instruments (clarinets, saxophones, oboes, bassoons) belong to this family of wood instruments. Not all woodwinds are made of wood (saxophones are made of brass, for example).

TIPCODE LIST

The Tipcodes in this book offer easy access to short videos, sound files, and other additional information at www.tipbook.com. For your convenience, the Tipcodes in this Tipbook have been listed below.

Tipcode	Topic	Page	Chapter
Kids-001	A tuning fork	73	4
Kids-002	Scales, cords, and arpeggios	82	4
Kids-003	A scale on piano	134	7
Kids-004	Four clarinet voices	136	7
Kids-005	A violin and a viola	155	9
Kids-006	Various styles of music on violin	155	9
Kids-007	Various styles of music on cello	155	9
Kids-008	The double bass	155	9
Kids-009	Nylon-string and steel-string guitars	155	9
Kids-010	Guitar effects	157	9
Kids-011	Various bass guitar sounds	157	9
Kids-012	Flute fantasy	160	9
Kids-013	Piccolo fantasy	160	9
Kids-014	Four clarinet voices	160	9
Kids-015	Soprano saxophone	160	9
Kids-016	Alto saxophone	160	9
Kids-017	Tenor saxophone	160	9
Kids-018	Baritone saxophone	160	9
Kids-019	Oboe and bassoon	161	9
Kids-020	Trumpet and flugelhorn	162	9
Kids-021	The piano	166	9
Kids-022	A five-piece drum set	169	9

WANT TO KNOW MORE?

There's much information available on all the subjects covered in this book, and the following pages offer a selection of helpful books, Websites, and organizations. These listings are not intended to be exhaustive; the information is current as of the publish date of this book.

Books

A random list of books on musical games, practice, music education, and related subjects:

- *Babies Make Music*, Lynn Kleiner (Alfred Publishing Company, 2000; 40 pages, ISBN 0-76929-407-3)
- *Musical Games, Fingerplays and Rhythmic Activities for Early Childhood*, Marian Wirth (Parker Publishing Company, 1983; 224 pages; ISBN 0-13607-085-X)
- *101 Rhythm Instrument Activities for Young Children*, Abigail Flesch Connors (Gryphon House, 2004; 128 pages; ISBN 0-87659-290-6)
- *Nurturing Your Child with Music: How Sound Awareness Creates Happy, Smart, and Confident Children*, John M. (Ortiz Beyond Words Publishing, 1999; 219 pages; ISBN 1-58270-021-4)
- *Music with the Brain in Mind*, Eric Jensen (Brain Store Inc, 2000; 110 pages; ISBN 1-89046-006-0)
- *Your Musical Child – Inspiring Kids to Play and Sing for Keeps*, Jessica Baron Turner, M.A. (String Letter Publishing, 2004; 240 pages; ISBN 1-890490-51-2)
- *The Young Musician's Survival Guide – Tips from Teens & Pros*, Amy Nathan (Oxford University Press, 2000; 128 pages; ISBN 0-19-512612-2)
- *The Practicing Revolution: Getting Great Results from the*

Six Days Between Music Lessons, Philip Johnston (PracticeSpot Press, 2002; 324 pages; ISBN 0-9581905-0-X)
- *Not Until You've Done Your Practice*, Phillip Johnston and David Sutton (FuturePerfect, 2000; 118 pages; ISBN 0-646-40265-X)
- *Practice Is a Dirty Word; How to Clean Up Your Act*, Ruth Bonetti (Words & Music; 106 pages)
- *A Parent's Guide to Band and Orchestra*, Jim Probasco (Betterway Publications, Inc., 1991; ISBN 1-55870-183-4; 136 pages)
- *A Parent's Guide to Teaching Music*, Jim Probasco (Betterway Publications, Inc., 1992; ISBN 1-55870-240-7; 136 pages)

General information
The following Websites offer lots of additional information and articles on a wide variety of subjects. Links to related sites are often included:
- National Association for Music Education / MENC
  www.menc.org
- American Music Conference
  www.amc-music.com, www.amc-music.org
- International Society for Music Education / ISME
  www.isme.org
- Music Teacher National Association / MTNA
  www.mtna.org
- Music Education Online
  www.childrensmusicworkshop.com
- Music Education Coalition
  www.supportmusic.com
- The Children's Music Network
  www.cmnonline.org
- Musicians United for Songs in the Classroom / M.U.S.I.C.
  www.twinblues.com
- National Federation of Music Clubs / NFMC
  www. nfmc-music.org
- M.I.N.D. Institute
  www.mindinst.org
- Parenting Central
  www.parenting-baby.com
- National Band Association
  www.nationalbandassoc.org

- National Association for Jazz Education
  www.iaje.org
- Music Council of Australia
  www.mca.org.au
- Music. Play for Life
  www.mca.org.au/music.playforlife.htm
- Australian Music Association
  www.australianmusic.asn.au
- Australian Children's Music Foundation
  www.acmf.com.au
- Australian Society for Music Education / ASME
  www.asme.edu.au
- Music Education New Zealand Aotearoa / MENZA
  (formerly NZSME)
  www.menza.org.nz
- Institute of Registered Music Teachers of New Zealand
  www.irmt.org.nz
- Pay the Piper
  www.paythepiper.co.uk
- Your Child and Music
  www.bbc.co.uk

Music advocacy

For information on music advocacy, visit:
- American Music Conference
  www.amc-music.com, www.amc-music.org
- Music Education Online
  www.childrensmusicworkshop.com
- Music Education Coalition
  www.supportmusic.com
- National Endowment for the Arts
  www.arts.endow.gov
- Save the Music Foundation
  www.vh1.com/partners/save_the_music
- Music Council of Australia
  www.mca.org.au

Websites for kids and teens (and you)
- The Music Edge
  www.themusicedge.com
- Children's Music Web
  www.childrensmusic.org

- Kid's Music Web
  www.kidsmusicweb.com
- Sesame Workshop Online Music Center
  www.sesameworkshop.com/sesamestreet/music/zone
- Musical Mouseum
  www.kididdles.com/mouseum

Information for disabled musicians
- E-bility.com, Arts and Disability
  www.e-bility.com/links/arts.php
- Coalition for Disabled Musicians, Inc.
  www.disabled-musicians.org
- Disabled Drummers Association
  www.disableddrummers.org
- Handidrummed.com
  www.handidrummed.com
- Drake Music Project
  www.drakemusicproject.org
- Music and the Deaf
  www.matd.org.uk

Examination boards
- Associated Board of Royal Schools of Music / ABRSM
  www.abrsm.org
- Royal American Conservatory Examinations
  www.royalamericanconservatory.org
- New York State School Music Association
  www.nyssma.org
- Royal Conservatory of Music
  www.rcmexaminations.org
- Trinity-Guildhall
  www.trinitycollege.co.uk
- The Australian Music Examinations Board / AMEB
  www.ameb.edu.au
- Australian and New Zealand Cultural Arts Limited /
  ANZCA
  www.anzca.com.au

Finding teachers and music schools
The following organizations can help you locate music
schools and private instrumental and vocal teachers:
- The National Guild of Community Schools of the Arts
  www.nationalguild.org

- Music Teachers National Association
  www.mtna.org
- Directory of Nationally Certified Teachers of Music
  https://members.mtna.org/mtnareports/
  Teacher@Lookup.asp
- American String Teachers Association
  www.astaweb.com
- VoiceTeachers.com
  www.voiceteachers.com
- National Association of Teachers of Singing
  www.nats.org
- Music Lessons Now
  www.musiclessonsonline.co.uk
- Musicians Friend
  www.musiciansfriend.co.uk
- Incorporated Society of Musicians
  www.ism.org
- National Association of Music Educators
  name2.org.uk
- Australian Music Teachers Register
  www.amtr.com.au
- Australian Directory of Music and Speech Teachers
  www.musicteachers.com.au
- Australian music teacher associations: Victorian MTA
  vmta.org.au
- Western Australia MTA, South Australian MTA,
  Tasmanian MTA, Queensland MTA, New South Wales
  MTA.

You can also consult the following special interest Websites:
- PrivateLessons.com
  www.privatelessons.com
- MusicStaff.com
  www.musicstaff.com
- The Music Teachers List
  www.teachlist.com
- Private Music Instructor National Directory
  www.oberwerk.com/pmind)

Miscellaneous
- Little Kids Rock: provides free lessons and instruments
  in public elementary schools.
  www.littlekidsrock.org

- Guitars in the Classroom: promotes guitar programs in schools.
  www.guitarsintheclassroom.com
- Caras Band Aid Program: provides grants to Canadian schools.
  www.carasonline.ca
- Youth Music: facilitates music making for children and teens.
  www.youthmusic.org.uk

THE TIPBOOK SERIES

Tipbook Music for Kids and Teens is the fifteenth volume of the Tipbook Series. The series is comprised of eleven books on musical instruments, including the singing voice, in addition to *Tipbook Music on Paper*, and *Tipbook Amplifiers and Effects*. Every Tipbook is a highly accessible and easy-to-read compilation of the knowledge and expertise of numerous musicians, teachers, technicians, and other experts, written for musicians — and their parents — at all levels, and in any style of music. Tipbooks can be read by children age ten and up (but they're also used by advanced players and their music teachers!).

Tipbook Music on Paper

Tipbook Music on Paper – Basic Theory offers everything you need to read and understand the language of music. The book presumes no prior understanding of theory and begins with the basics, explaining standard notation, but moves on to advanced topics such as odd time signatures and transposing music in a fashion that makes things really easy to understand. It's also a handy reference, and the 4"x8" Tipbook format allows you to take it anywhere you go.

Instrument Tipbooks

The Instrument Tipbooks each offer a wealth of highly accessible, yet well-founded information on one or more closely related instruments. The first chapters of each

Tipbook explain the very basics of the instrument(s), explaining all the parts and what they do, describing what's involved in learning to play, and indicating typical instrument prices. The core chapters, addressed to advanced players as well, turn you into an instant expert on the instrument. This knowledge allows you to make an informed purchase and get the most out of your instrument. Comprehensive chapters on maintenance, intonation, and tuning are also included, as well a brief section on the history, the family, and the production of the instrument.

Tipbook Violin and Viola, Tipbook Cello

The Tipbooks on orchestral strings cover a wide range of subjects, ranging from an explanation of different types of tuning pegs, fine tuners, and tailpieces, to how body dimen-
sions and the bridge may influence the instrument's timbre. Tips on how to audition instruments and bows are included. Special chapters are dedicated to the characteristics of different types of strings, bows, and rosins, allowing you to get the most out of the instrument.

Tipbook Piano

Choosing a piano becomes a lot easier with the knowledge provided in *Tipbook Piano*, which makes for a better understanding of this complex, expensive instrument without going into too much detail. How to judge and compare piano keyboards and pedals, the influence of the instrument's dimensions, different types of cabinets, how to judge an instrument's timbre, the difference between laminated and solid wood soundboards, accessories, hybrid and digital pianos, and why tuning and regulation are so important: Everything is covered in this handy guide.

Tipbook Acoustic Guitar

Tipbook Acoustic guitar explains all elements that make for a good instrument, and helps

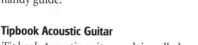

you recognize and judge a guitar's timbre, performance, and playability. Of course there are dedicated chapters on different types of strings and their characteristics, on changing and cleaning strings, on tuning, and even on how to best maintain your fingernails.

Tipbook Electric Guitar & Bass Guitar

Electric guitars and bass guitars come in many shapes and sizes. This book explains all their features and characteristics, from neck profiles, frets, and types of wood to different types of pickups, tuning machines, and — of course — strings. Tuning and advanced do-it-yourself intonation techniques are included.

Tipbook Flute & Piccolo

Flute prices range from a few hundred to fifty thousand dollars and more. *Tipbook Flute and Piccolo* tells you how workmanship, materials, and other elements make for different instruments with vastly different prices, and teaches you how to find the instrument that best suits your or your child's

needs. Open-hole or closed-hole keys, a B-foot or a C-foot, split-E or donut, inline or offset G? You'll be able to answer all these questions — and more — after reading this guide.

Tipbook Saxophone

At first glance, all alto saxophones look alike. And all tenor saxophones do too — yet they all play and sound different from each other. *Tipbook Saxophone* discusses the instrument in detail, explaining the key system and the use of additional keys, the different types of pads, corks, and springs, mouthpieces and

how they influence timbre and playability, reeds (and how to select and adjust them) and much more.

Tipbook Clarinet

Tipbook Clarinet sheds light on every element of this fascinating instrument. The knowledge presented in this guide makes selecting and auditioning a clarinet much easier, and you will be an instant expert on the pros and cons of offset and in-line trill keys, rounded or French-style keys, and all other aspects of the instrument. Special chapters are dedicated to reeds (selecting, testing, and adjusting reeds), mouthpieces and ligatures, and maintenance.

Tipbook Trumpet & Trombone, Flugelhorn & Cornet

The Tipbook on brass instruments focuses on the smaller horns listed in the title. It explains all jargon you come across when you're out to buy or rent an instrument, from bell material to the shape of the bore, the leadpipe, valves and valve slides, and all other elements of the horn. Mouthpieces, a crucial choice for the sound and playability of all brasswinds, are covered in a separate chapter.

Tipbook Drums

A drum is a drum is a drum? Not true — and this book tells you all the ins and outs of their differences, from the type of wood to the dimensions of the shell, the shape of the bearing edge, and the drum's hardware. Special chapters discuss selecting drum sticks, drum heads, and cymbals. Tuning and muffling, two techniques a drummer must

master to make the instrument sound as good as it can, are covered in detail, providing step-by-step instructions.

Tipbook Keyboard & Digital Piano

Buying a home keyboard or a digital piano may find you confronted with numerous unfamiliar terms. *Tipbook Keyboard & Digital Piano* explains all of them in a very easy-to-read fashion — from hammer action and non-weighted keys to MIDI, layers and splits, arpeggiators and sequencers, expression pedals and multi-switches, and more, including special chapters on how to judge the instrument's sound, accompaniment systems, and the various types of connections these instruments offer.

Tipbook Vocals – The Singing Voice

Tipbook Vocals –The Singing Voice helps you realize the full potential of your singing voice. The book, written in close collaboration with classical and non-classical singers and teachers, allows you to discover the world's most personal and precious instrument without reminding you of anatomy class.

Topics include breathing and breath support, singing loudly without hurting your voice, singing in tune, the timbre of your voice, articulation, registers and ranges, memorizing lyrics, and more. The main purpose of the dedicated chapter on voice care is to prevent negative symptoms.

Tipbook Amplifiers & Effects

Whether you need a guitar amp, a sound system, a multi-effects unit for a bass guitar, or a keyboard amplifier, *Tipbook Amplifiers & Effects* helps you make a good choice. Two chapters explain general features (controls, equalizers, speakers, MIDI, etc.) and figures (watts, ohms, impedance, etc.), and further chapters cover the specifics of guitar amps,

bass amps, keyboard amps, acoustic amps, and sound systems. Effects and effect units are dealt with in detail, and there are dedicated chapters on microphones and pickups, and cables and wireless systems.

International editions

The Tipbook Series is also available in Spanish, French, German, Dutch, Swedish, and (as of 2006) Chinese.

INDEX

Please see the glossary on pages 00*–00* for additional definitions of the terms used in this book.

A

Absolute pitch: 123
Accordion: 133, 151, 168
Acoustic guitar: 76, 101, 102, 131, 138, 155–156, 157
ACT, American College Test: 28
Action songs: 21
Adult teeth: 13
Advocacy: 29, 187
Affiliations: 43
Aptitude tests: 121
Armchair memorizing: 92
Arpeggio: 82
Assigning instruments: 121–122
Athletic band: 143
Awards: 96

B

Background brass: 131, 163
Balalaika: 158, 159
Band instruments: 182
Banjo: 149, 150, 151, 158
Baritone: 55, 131, 145, 164
Baritone saxophone: 104, 149, 160
Bass drum: 168
Bass guitar: 48, 148, 157
Bassoon: 31, 52, 53, 102, 161, 119
Big band: 149
Bongos: 151
Borrowing instruments: 103–104
Bowed instruments: See *String instruments.*
BPM (Beats Per Minute): 67, 87
Braces: 13, 53–55
Brass bands: 145
Brasswinds: 54–55, 103, 123–124, 161–166
Buy-back plans: 108

C

Celtic harp: 132
Chamber ensemble: 146
Chamber orchestra: 146
Children's instruments: 24, 126–133
Choir: 34, 56, 135
Chord diagrams: 9, 50, 51
Chord: 64
Clarinet: 52, 54, 76, 77, 101, 114, 129, 159, 160
Community music schools: 35
Competitions: 43, 62, 144
Computer: 14, 27, 74, 171–172
Concert band: 142
Congas: 151, 170
Conservatory: 27
Contract: 96
Cornet: 130, 136, 145

D

Digital piano: 75, 78, 112, 166, 167
Dixieland: 149
DJ: 149
Double bass: 76, 126, 133, 154, 155
Double horn: 131
Double-jointed fingers: 125
Double-reed instruments: 161
Down-sized instruments: 126–133
Drum and bugle corps: 144
Drum corps: 144
Drum set: 79, 103, 132, 150, 168, 169
Drums: 168
Dynamics: 10

E

E♭-clarinet: *129*
E♭-flute: *128*
Ear training: *24, 182*
Early childhood music programs: *24–26*
Easy instruments: *128, 134–136*
Electric cello: *157*
Electric guitar:
Electric violin: *78, 157–158*
Electronic drum set: *79*
Electronic tuner: *73*
Embouchure: *128, 161*
English horn: *161*
Euphonium: *131, 145, 164*
Examination boards: *58–59, 188*
Exams: *58–62*
Exploratory courses: *119*

F

Field drums: *143, 168*
Financial aid: *35, 36, 116*
Fingering: *9, 89*
Flugelhorn: *130, 136, 145, 162*
Flute: *52, 54, 77, 119, 124, 125–126, 128–129, 160*
Folk guitar: *132, 156*
Folk harp: *132*
Fractional sizes: *12, 105, 106, 131*
French horn: *31, 55, 131, 127, 162*
Frets: *154*
Fretted instruments: See *String instruments.*
Full orchestra: *144*
Fusion: *149*

G

Getting the most out of lessons: *45–48*
Gifted children: *57*
Glockenspiel: *170*
Graded music exams: *58–62*

Grants: *29, 190*
Group lessons: *31–34*
Guitar: *4, 15, 21, 27, 101, 125, 131–132, 148, 155–156*

H

Harp: *132–133, 158*
Headphones: *75–76, 77, 80, 166*
Hearing protection: *80–81*
Home keyboard: *20, 49, 126, 135, 167*
Home school music programs: *30*
Home studios: *34*
Hybrid piano: *78*

I

Independent music lessons: *30–31*
Instrument prices: *102–103*

J

Jazz orchestra: *149*
Jazz: *149, 150*

K

Keyboard instruments: *166–168*
Kindermusik: *25*
Kodaly: *25*

L

Learning styles: *14–17*
Leasing an instrument: *104–108*
Left-handed instruments: *125*
Lesson fees: *35–36*
Lesson times: *35*
Lever harp: *132*

M

Mallet instruments: *170*
Mandolin: *158*
Marching band: *143*

Marimba: *170*
Melodic percussion: *170*
Melody instruments: *45, 137*
Memorizing music: *89-92*
Method-centered teachers: *41*
Metronome: *73*
Mock auditions: *175-176*
Mouth harp: *168*
Mozart effect: *3*
Music advocacy: *29, 187*
Music education programs: *24-26*
Music for Young Children: *25*
Music readiness programs: *24*
Music schools: *34-35*
Music stores, types of: *109-110*
Music Together: *25*

N

New piece, practicing: *87-89*
Noise, how to reduce –: *75-80*
Notebook: *44*
Nylon-string guitar: *131, 155, 156*

O

Oboe: *31, 52, 76, 77, 102, 119, 129-130, 159, 161*
Off days: *97*
Orchestra bells: *170*
Orchestral instruments: *182*
Orchestral strings: *182*
Orff Schulwerk: *25*
Organ: *137, 166, 167*

P

Pedal harp: *132, 158*
Pep band: *143*
Percussion instruments: *22, 132, 135, 143, 144, 168, 170-171*
Perfect pitch: *123*
Philharmonic orchestra: *145*
Physical features: *121-122, 123-126*

Piano: *4, 12, 76, 78, 113, 120, 132, 166*
Piccolo: *129, 160*
Pit percussion: *144*
Pitch: *10, 19, 73, 122-123*
Practice, how long should you –: *65-67*
Practicing a new piece: *87-89*
Practicing techniques: *86-87*
Practicing, structure: *84-86*
Practicing, when: *68-71*
Practicing, where: *71-74*
Practicing: *63-92*
Pre-birth: *9-10*
Private instruction: *31-33*
Private lessons: *31-33*
Progress, lack of –: *18-19, 39, 98, 99*
Pull-out lessons: *28*

R

Reading music: *3, 12, 25, 49-50, 8, 97*
Recorder: *52, 102, 127-128, 159*
Recording lessons: *46-47*
Recording practice sessions: *71, 176*
Recreational music making: *64-65*
Reed instruments: *113, 160, 161, 183*
Relative pitch: *122*
Renting an instrument: *104-108*
Rent-to-own: *106*
Rent-to-rent: *106*
Rewards: *60, 69, 85, 95-96*

S

Sample: *166*
SAT, Scholastic Assessment Test: *3, 28*
Saxhorn: *164*
Saxonett: *129*
Saxophone: *78, 102, 119, 129, 134, 160*

Saz: *158–159*
Scale: *82*
School music programs: *26–30*
Scramble bands: *145*
Secondhand instruments:
     111–113
shadow practicing: *92*
Shakers: *10, 168*
Show band: *143*
Sight-reading: *56, 83*
Singing: *10, 12, 20, 34, 135*
Single horn: *131*
Single-reed instruments: *160*
Snare drum: *168*
Soprano brass: *163*
Sound level: *75–80*
Special needs, children with –:
     43, 56–57
Stand band: *143*
Steel-string guitar: *132, 155*
String bass: *76*
String instruments: *153–159*
Stringed instruments: *153–159*
Strings: *144, 153*
Strolling strings: *144*
Student-centered teachers: *41*
Studio policy: *44, 45, 46*
Summer sessions: *47*
Suzuki method: *25*
Switching instruments: *14, 107,*
     120, 122, 136
Symphonic band: *142*
Symphonic winds: *142*
Symphony orchestra:
Synthesizer: *167*

T

Tablature: *51*
Talents and abilities: *19–20,*
     122–123
Teacher qualifications: *42–43*
Teacher, assessing a –: *42–45*
Teacher, learning without a –:
     48–51
Teacher, seeking a –: *37*

Teeth: *51–55*
Tenor drums: *169*
Tenor horn: *131, 164*
Timbales: *151, 170*
Timbre: *111*
Timp toms: *169*
Timpani: *144, 168, 170*
Toms: *168*
Toy instruments: *10*
Treble brass: *163*
Trombone: *76, 126, 130–131,*
     163
Trumpet: *52, 55, 77, 125, 130,*
161, 162
Tuba: *104, 131, 163–164*
Turntable: *172*

U

Ukulele: *132*
Upright bass: *76*
Used instruments: *111–113*

V

Varsity band: *143*
Vibraphone: *170*
Viola: *126, 155*

W

Wind band: *26, 142*
Wind ensemble: *142*
Wind instruments: *13, 52, 127*
Wind orchestra: *142*
Wind symphony: *142*
Woodwinds instruments:
     159–161

X

Xylophone: *10, 170*

Y

Yoga: *179*

ESSENTIAL DATA

Four pages for essential information on band directors, music teachers, instruments, and so on.

Name Child:

Band/orchestra director:

Email: Phone:

Music teacher:

Email: Phone:

Instrumental teacher:

Email: Phone:

Music school

Email: Phone:

Music store:

Email: Phone:

Name Child:

Band/orchestra director:

Email: Phone:

Music teacher:

Email: Phone:

Instrumental teacher:

Email: Phone:

Music school

Email: Phone:

Music store:

Email: Phone:

Name Child:

Band/orchestra director:

Email: Phone:

Music teacher:

Email: Phone:

Instrumental teacher:

Music school

Email: Phone:

Music store:

Email: Phone:

Name Child:

Band/orchestra director:

Email: Phone:

Music teacher:

Email: Phone:

Instrumental teacher:

Email: Phone:

Music school

Email: Phone:

Music store:

Email: Phone:

INFORMATIVE WEBSITES

Organization	URL
	www.
	www.
	www.
	www.
	www.
	www.
	www.

INSTRUMENT DATA

In the event of one of your children's instruments being stolen or lost, or
if you want to sell it, it's useful to have the following data at hand.

Instrument 1

Make and model:

Serial number:

Color:

Date of purchase:

Price:

Purchased from:

Email: Phone:

Instrument 2

Make and model:

Serial number:

Color:

Date of purchase:

Price:

Purchased from:

Email: Phone:

Instrument 3

Make and model:

Serial number:

Color:

Date of purchase:

Price:

Purchased from:

Email: Phone:

Instrument 4

Make and model:

Serial number:

Color:

Date of purchase:

Price:

Purchased from:

Email: Phone:

REEDS, STRINGS, STICKS...

It can be helpful to list the reeds, strings, drum sticks, or other accessories that your child is currently using to make re-ordering much simpler.

Brand:

Type:

Other details:

Brand:

Type:

Other details:

Brand:

Type:

Other details:

Brand:

Type:

Other details:

Brand:

Type:

Other details:

Brand:

Type:

Other details:

TIPBOOK SERIES
MUSIC AND MUSICAL INSTRUMENTS
Released

Tipbook Acoustic Guitar
Tipbook Amplifiers & Effects
Tipbook Cello
Tipbook Clarinet
Tipbook Drums
Tipbook Electric Guitar & Bass Guitar
Tipbook Flute & Piccolo
Tipbook Keyboard & Digital Piano
Tipbook Music for Kids and Teens
Tipbook Music on Paper – Basic Theory
Tipbook Piano
Tipbook Saxophone
Tipbook Trumpet & Trombone
Tipbook Violin & Viola
Tipbook Vocals

Want to know what's available today?
Take a look at www.tipbook.com.